Radium Halos

(Senseless Series, Book 1)

By W.J. May

Copyright 2014 W.J. May

D1518932

Also by W.J. May

Hidden Secrets Saga
Seventh Mark - Part 1
Seventh Mark - Part 2

The Chronicles of Kerrigan
Rae of Hope
Dark Nebula

The Senseless Series
Radium Halos

Standalone
Five Shades of Fantasy
Glow - A Young Adult Fantasy Sampler
Shadow of Doubt - Part 1
Shadow of Doubt - Part 2
Four and a Half Shades of Fantasy

The Senseless Series:

Download Radium Halos part 1 For FREE

Radium Halos part 2 – coming February 2014

Website: http://www.wanitamay.yolasite.com
Facebook:
https://www.facebook.com/pages/Author-WJ-May-FAN-PAGE
Cover design by: Book Cover by Design
Book II – Coming 2014

Chapter 1

Zoe

I hated the mine. Like a crypt across the horizon, the place always made me shudder. They had closed it down years ago and boarded up the entrance. The horror-film image still haunted me.

Tonight vehicles littered the overgrown grass field surrounding the shaft. From behind the orange and yellow flames of a bonfire, blue spirits danced about, as if the mine had allowed them to escape. Foreboding lingered in the pit of my stomach. The sound of music, chatter, and laughter barely muted the feeling.

I shifted away from the fire and dropped my head against the back of the lawn chair. Ominous clouds created large voids in the dotted, glittery sky. *To rain or not to rain, that is the question.*

Heidi waved a hand back and forth in front of my face. "Earth to Zoe. Earth to Zoe. Come back to Elliot Lake. The school bonfire is missing you."

Even with my eyes cast toward the sky, I could hear the smile in her voice. I grinned and turned to face my best bud, one last shutter sneaking up my spine. "The mine gives me the creeps."

Heidi leaned over on her lawn chair and nudged me with her elbow. "I heard that back in the sixties or seventies, half the miners ended up with some toxic disease from the uranium. Most likely cancer."

Rylee, my other best friend, tossed her dark hair over her shoulder and rolled her eyes. "Only you two would come up with the number one way to kill a mood. The big 'C'."

"It's not like we're going inside." I stuck my tongue out and tried to keep the corners of my mouth from turning up. Pretending to copy Rylee's hair toss, I swung my head dramatically and let my recently straightened blonde strands flip around. Not near as sexy or smooth as Rylee's. I glanced at Heidi, unable to mimic the action. "I still can't believe you cut your hair so short."

"I donated it. Totally worth it."

"Yeah. I'm cool with that, but it's been long since third grade."

Rylee stepped over and touched the back of Heidi's hair. "The shaved part at the back is incredible."

I lacked the nerve to do something so daring. "It's awesome."

"It's what I wanted ever since I saw it in a mag," Heidi said.

Our little pixie. The new cut took away some of her innocent look—making her appear older. I liked it. It represented the change of our final year of high school. We were growing up.

"...but dying it platinum." Rylee whistled. "I bet your mom had a coronary when you got home."

Heidi grinned a tiny bit. "She was pretty ticked." Her tiny fingers flicked the spiked front.

"Soooo..." Rylee straightened in her chair, causing her chest to stick out. *Uh oh, prowl pose. Rylee's on a hot man hunt.* Rylee pressed a perfectly manicured hand against her flat belly. "Brent said there's a new guy in town."

I got up and moved to Brent, who'd been sitting on a tree stump quietly playing his guitar. The humungous mine silhouetted behind him. It looked like a monster's mouth trying to swallow him and everything around it up. *Stop being such a scaredy-cat.* I rolled my eyes heavenward to clear my overactive imagination and focused on Brent.

He sat with his head down while he strummed along to the music blaring from the speakers. In the firelight, his brown hair appeared sandy-blonde. As if sensing my gaze, he glanced up. A smile touched his lips, and his eyes seemed to twinkle from the reflection of the dancing flames.

"Where's Seth?" I realized Mr. Clean, our fifth partner in crime, hadn't shown up yet.

"He's bringing fresh meat." Brent continued playing while the stereo music blared behind us. He managed to make his composition sound perfectly in tune, and yet totally different than the rock song playing.

"Ohhh... I love hot dogs and burgers!" Heidi sat down by Brent. "Topped off with marshmallows for s'mores, of course."

"No, silly, not food. Nice hair crop, by the way." Brent ruffled the back of her head. "There's a new kid in town. He's from England or Ireland, somewhere across the pond."

Rylee, always gorgeous and perky, swept her black hair up in a pony and then dropped it perfectly into place. "Tall, hot, and handsome, I hope."

"Like me, huh?" Brent laughed.

"How come no one knew he was coming?" Rylee played with her car keys, a little green dot flashing as she tapped a button on them. "This town's so small. Everyone should've been talking about it over the summer holidays." She started pacing around the fire, scouting the small crowd.

"Guess it was like a last minute decision. I'm sure you'll find out all the details when you devour him." Brent laughed and played two loud *boom chukka bings* punctuated by a clap on his guitar.

Heidi covered a smile with her hand. I faked a cough. We both knew what Rylee's response would be.

She made her signature baby-pout face. "I don't eat men. I simply get bored."

"Put the lip away. It's not gonna work." I grinned. *Only Rylee could be Rylee.* "We always get stuck picking up the pieces after you've broken the poor guy's heart." I bent forward, pretending to pick up a million invisible pieces of shattered heart off the ground.

Rylee had dated every boy in our class, plus a grade or two above, since starting high school. She wasn't a tramp. Every decent guy in town just wanted to see if he might be Mr. Right. "How 'bout tonight you give the new guy a chance to breathe? Not make him your next conquest right away?"

"Conquest?" Rylee raised her eyebrows.

"You know," Heidi said, sarcasm dripping. "What you do all summer long with the vacationers?"

"I get it. You don't like competing." Rylee shrugged. "I figured you guys thought it was fun."

"Not when we lose all the time." I sighed. "Kinda hard to compete against your midnight black hair and perfect voluptuous body. Makes the boys of summer migrate toward you." Heidi and I didn't stand a chance, even when Rylee didn't try to get them. *I'm not jealous.* How could you fight nature? *Okay, maybe a teeny bit jealous.*

A loud boom suddenly rocked the air. I jumped and whirled around to see where the noise came from. Startled at first, everyone around the fire laughed when they realized the noise came from above.

"That didn't sound good." Brent set his guitar in its case lying on the ground.

"Maybe it'll just pass over. There's no forecast for rain," Rylee said.

Heidi pointed toward the other side of the bonfire. "Well, if it does start pouring, we're on the wrong side. Everyone's going to make a mad dash for their cars, and we picked the furthest spot. We're like a kilometre away."

"Great." I grimaced. Getting wet meant my straightened hair would turn curly and, worse, the dreaded frizzies.

Brent picked up his guitar case. "No way am I letting this baby get ruined. I bought it in an antique shop in Germany. Had to carry it around with me for the last two weeks in Europe."

"We'll be fine. It's not gonna rain. The skies—" Rylee paused and glanced up. "Whoa, those are freakin' huge, black clouds!"

As if to mock her, the sky lit up with a zigzag flash of lightning, immediately followed by a sonic boom that shook the ground. Large raindrops splattered down, making the fire hiss in protest. Everyone started to grab chairs and food and belongings. Over the shrieks of the girls, someone hollered to head over to the bowling alley and continue the party there.

Brent grabbed Heidi's and Rylee's arms. "Come on. We can hang out in the mine until the storm blows over. It's closer than our cars." He let go of the girls, shrugged his guitar case over his shoulder, and took off running toward the mine.

I flinched. The idea of going into the spooky, old, abandoned mine didn't sound like the best plan. I stood by the sizzling fire, getting drenched.

I could feel my hair curling against my neck. "Might as well join him. You all handed your cell phones into the pot for the game student council planned later on. I'm probably the only one who didn't." I held my hand above my eyes to shield some of the rain.

Rylee giggled. "This should be interesting." She grabbed Heidi's sleeve and they took off running. I followed slightly behind.

The rain came in torrents and the long grass became slippery. Despite the wetness, I upped my pace—which only made me stumble.

Lightning ripped through the sky again, illuminating the mine opening. The entrance seemed to transform into a gruesome face made of earth, ready to swallow us up. Even the trees surrounding the mine looked like hands trying to grasp and pull the doorway under. I hesitated, even though I knew it was just the shadows and light playing with my mind.

I walked the last twenty yards along the old, half-buried rail tracks and came to a halt behind Rylee and Heidi. Brent must have pried off the large slab of wood, which had boarded up the entrance to the abandoned mine. *He's desperate. He's always careful with his hands.* The missing board created a crawl space just large enough for us to get inside.

Rylee disappeared though the hole, and I caught Heidi hesitating. I looked toward where my car should be parked. *Completely hidden by the rain.* Noah's ark could float by and we'd never see it.

"Go on. I'm right behind you," I said.

She slipped though and vanished into its darkness. Dropping down, I crept through the sinister hole.

Another crackle of thunder rattled the wooden boards and echoed down into the mine. It was darker than dark inside, except for the light cast by the small opening. Through the broken gap, the last remains of the bonfire disappeared in a cloud of smoke.

"Holy crap! Where the heck did *that* come from?" Brent's voice sounded further down the tunnel, and lower, as if he was on his knees.

"This place reeks like rotten eggs," I complained. "Can't see a thing."

A small beam of light appeared on a nearby wall and found its way to Brent's face. "Hey, cut that out." He blinked and held an arm up. "Who's doing that?"

"Me." Rylee giggled. "My keychain has one of those tiny flashlights you use to find your ignition in the dark." She flashed the light onto her scrunched-up face and made a spooky ghost sound, "Oooooooo."

"You're not scary." Brent laughed. "You sound like a little kid. Maybe someone a little more mature should be holding it."

Rylee shifted the yellow light to Heidi's face. "It's not much, but at least we can shine it on any bats that try to bite us. Or maybe there're spiders and other creepy crawly things." She moved the light around the dirt walls, zigzagging and making circles.

"Bats? Spiders?" Heidi squealed. "I'm not moving from this spot –and keep those vermin away from me." You couldn't miss the shudder in her voice. Rylee flashed the light in Heidi's direction again. We stood on a slope, with Brent at the lowest end.

"We'll be fine." Brent wrapped his arm around Heidi. "This thing's going to blow over in a bit. Wind and rain that fast and heavy can't last long."

We followed Rylee's little light as she made patterns on the dirt-covered wall.

I kept quiet and shifted my weight from foot to foot. My sneakers were soaked from the wet grass, making loud sucking sounds as I moved around. My friends grumbled as they moved. *Dirt walls, dirt floor and musty stinkin' dirt roof.* I scowled as cold wet filled my shoe and ran over top of it. "Great. If you guys haven't noticed, this downpour's created a small mud current running over my shoes. I don't exactly fancy swimming in a river of mud down through this godforsaken mine." *Definitely not a good idea.*

As if the weather mocked our predicament, another bolt of lightning lit the opening and a howl of wind blew more rain inside. The contrast after the shock of brilliant light made the mine opening even blacker. Thunder threatened to shake the dirt ceiling. An iridescent beam flashed across my eyes and then bounced off the frightened faces of my friends and slowly traced down a crack on the side wall. Four pairs of eyes followed Rylee's little flashlight.

A blast of cold air followed by a stream of water coursed into the opening. It pushed against my calves. "Shit!" escaped from my lips before I could stop it. *Freakin' freezing!* As my footing started to slip, I grabbed for whoever was close enough to help keep me from landing on my butt. My fingers found cotton and some kind of strong material. I clenched tightly, then realized I'd managed to grab the top of their jeans and my fingers now pressed against warm, taut abdominal muscles.

Strong hands gripped my arms and helped me upright. "You okay?" Brent's hot breath brushed against my ear.

"Yup... Th-Thanks." I swallowed. "You're lucky I didn't pull your pants down."

Brent chuckled. "We're going to have to move further in." His hand stayed on my forearm. "Zoe's about to go waterskiing and she'll take anyone down who's in front of her."

"I'm not stepping any further into this pit of darkness!" Heidi screeched. "There is NO way we're getting lost inside this tomb. What if some rabid animal bites us?"

Lightning erupted again, followed by a loud thick and deep shattering crack that sounded nothing like thunder. A massive crash shook the ground, which made me jump. From the splashing sounds around me, I wasn't the only one. I pivoted around toward the entrance of the mine. Rylee sloshed her way past me and flashed her little light on the dark opening.

You've got to be jokin'!

Instead of a small gap where we'd crawled through, a humungous fallen tree trunk covered it. Rylee shone the light around the gap again. She paused at the bottom. Water gushed into the mine, creating more of a mudslide around our feet and legs. It ran down the slope leading further into the darkness.

Brent muttered, "Ah, shit."

Heidi whimpered, but didn't cry out.

"We're trapped," I said, my heart slamming against my ribcage. "W-What the heck are we gonna do?"

A strange howl erupted further inside the mine and echoed off the walls. Rylee dropped her flashlight. Dark turned to pitch black.

Chapter 2

"What the hell was that?" Brent asked.

"Dammit!" Rylee swore, followed by splashing water.

"What're you doing?" I hated being in the pitch black. *I knew coming in here would be a mistake.*

"Trying to find my stupid keys. That flashlight better still work." More splashing and sloshing sounds echoed through the cave. "Got 'em!" Metal jingling together sounded like a little musical bell.

Thank goodness the key light came back on – dim but still beauty to my eyes. We moved closer together.

"Awwwweeeeeehhheee!" The strange noise from before sounded again—closer this time. Ringing inside my head intensified as my heart thundered against my ribcage.

"I-Is it s-some kinda animal?" Heidi pressed closer, pulling us all into a tighter circle.

Rylee released a nervous laugh. "Probably some old miner's ghost stuck in the mine. It's ticked we're in here."

"Gimme a break," I snapped, not meaning to. "Sorry. I don't want to be here."

"Awwwee—ow!"

What the—?

Brent straightened and stepped back toward a dirt wall. "No," his head shook as he spoke, "I'm gonna freakin' kill him." He took a step into the sloping mine. "Seth! Get your ass up here NOW!"

There was a moment of silence followed by booming laughter. Rylee turned the light further into the mine.

Seth appeared around the darkened corner two minutes later looking like Mr. Clean in his white short-sleeve tee shirt, faded blue jeans, and short cropped hair. *At least the top half's Mr. Clean.* His jeans and sneakers were covered in mud.

I skipped my gaze over to the tall, lean, dark-haired guy walking beside him. The complete opposite in dark jeans and black shirt 'The Beatles' emblazed with a Union Jack design on his chest. Even with Rylee's small light, his eyes matched his hair, their reflection dark against the dim light. His hands were stuffed into his back pockets and as he chuckled at something Seth muttered. I heard my own breath catch.

I couldn't stop staring. *Cute, very cute.* My heart sped up a few erratic beats as I wondered how his voice sounded. Then I remembered they'd just scared the crap out of us. "Seth, you're such a dill-weed. Poor Heidi's nearly peed her pants."

"Sorry," Seth said, his baritone voice echoing off the nearby walls. "We broke in here when the storm started. I hope I didn't scare you. We were just messing."

"It wasn't funny. At all," Heidi said.

"Sorry. We were just around the corner when we heard you guys crawl in." Seth craned his neck, trying to look behind us. "No one else?"

Brent stepped forward. "They all ran for their cars. Did you break the board at the entrance?"

"Yup." Seth grinned, flexing a massive arm muscle. "By the way, this is Kieran. He moved in down the street from me a couple of days ago."

"G'd ev'nin'." Kieran's low voice carried a thick accent. *English? Australian?*

Rylee sloshed over and hugged Seth and then Kieran. "I'm Rylee."

"Nice to meet you." Kieran politely stepped back.

Heidi waved a little hand, then reached for hair to play with out of habit. Not finding any with the new hairdo, she scratched her neck instead "I'm Heidi. Are you from England?"

"Och." He smiled and shook his head. "Not hardly. I'm from Inverness, a wee town in Scotland."

Brent nodded and held his hand out. Seth slapped the front, then back. The shake was their Boy Club greeting they'd made up in third grade and, sadly, still used it. "'Eh, Kieran. I'm Brent, the music man." He patted the guitar case on his back that I'd completely forgotten about. He hummed a few chords of "Auld Lang Syne."

Kieran grinned.

I stepped forward and inhaled trying to think of something witty to say. The deep breath killed all thought process and instead gave me the opportunity to breathe in Kieran's scent. *Probably some aftershave mixed with the Highland waters of Scotland.* Trying to appear cool, I crossed my right ankle over my left and nearly fell into the running water. Thank goodness for the dimness. "Hu-hello," I said, groaning inwardly at the rust in my husky voice. "I'm Zoe. Fancy meeting you in such a... a... memorable place."

"Speaking of which," Brent said. "Do you know a way outta here? Zoe seems to think we're trapped."

"We're not trapped." Seth pushed past us to the opening of the mine. Rylee shone her little light at the jammed entrance and we all moved closer to Seth. He spread his feet and squatted down to push against the tree trunk. Brent and Kieran joined him, their arms flexed with exertion against the pale flashlight.

"The tree's not... going to... budge." Seth grunted as he pushed harder. He lost his footing and crashed to his knees in the rushing water. "Crap." He grabbed Brent's outstretched hand and vaulted up, soaked to the waist. "There's a runoff rain spout by the mine opening, the tree must've took it down as it fell. That's why there's all this water running in here."

My teeth were nearly rattling out my head. I blinked in surprise, not realizing how cold I'd become. *Or maybe it's just the mine.* Or the fact that we were stuck here! I hated this place, but wasn't about to admit it out loud. Wringing my hands, I pressed my lips together to stop their trembling. Images of being forced into the deep, dark pits of the mine and never being found galloped through my head.

Seth reached toward Rylee. "Give me the light. We had one but it died after two minutes. We've already been in a ways and didn't find anything in the dark. I'll go further to see if there's a dryer place we can wait out the storm."

"I'm not moving from this spot." Heidi clutched my arm and pulled me tight against her. My shoe, half sucked into the bed, made me almost fall face-first into the cold water. *Great, mud-caked hair.*

"Seth's right," Kieran said. "We can't stay here. We'll be sliding down the mine on our arses." He splashed past to stand by Seth. "I'll come with you."

"Don't go," pleaded Heidi.

"I'll stay." Brent gave my shoulder a reassuring squeeze as he stepped between me and Heidi.

Rylee slipped by and stood on the other side of Heidi. "They have to look. If we're gonna be here all night, we can't stay here waiting to be rescued. Nobody even knows we came this way. They were all running for their cars."

"We should've done the same thing." *My gut was right before.*

In the semi-darkness, I watched Heidi collapse in tears against Rylee. Then two boys, and our only little light, disappeared into the darkness. Tears welled but, breathing deep, I fought them back down. We didn't need any more waterworks at the moment. It was dark, cold, and silent. My heart hammered and fear gnawed inside me.

Oh how I wanted to follow the guys. Instead, I patted Heidi's arm and moved a few steps away to try and find higher ground. Moving forward, I grimaced when water sloshed up to my knees. My arms reached out in the darkness to find the wall. Each step a hesitant move forward, I concentrated on not slipping.

The cool, dry dirt of the wall felt like heaven against my fingers. Sliding my foot forward, I felt higher ground against my sneaker. Another tentative step forward, using the wall for balance, I found a small ledge, wide enough to stand on. A tiny surge of hope pulsed through my veins.

"Over here," I called. "There's a raised part we can stand on till the guys get back."

"Here, take my arm, Heidi," Brent said.

Heidi was full-on crying now. Hiccups and everything. *Poor thing.*

They clambered onto the small rock shelf. We waited for what seemed like an eternity, none of us talking. Heidi managed to calm herself down on the higher ground. The howling wind and shattering thunder seemed to be having a conversation of its own.

I shifted my weight from foot to foot. *What time is it?* The little hands on my watch glowed faintly. Half past eleven—*already?*

"Think they're all right?" Rylee asked.

I opened my mouth to reply, when a *whoop* erupted from deeper inside the mine. All four of us jumped.

"Son of a bitch!" Brent swore as he slid and landed in the muddy water. "They better have found something."

Moments later, laughter and male voices drifted through the darkness of the mine toward us. The small, round light appeared. My tense posture slumped. A new knot between my shoulder blades burned. I tried to stretch my back out without slipping.

"We found a closed off room. It's nothing spectacular, but heaven compared to this. It's dry so we can hang out there for the night. There's like a glass dome thing on top, and when the lightning flashes, it brightens up the room." Seth swung the flashlight around, finally finding us lined against the wall. "What the? You guys in a police lineup?" He laughed. "Or are you prisoners, trying to dig your way out?"

"Shut up." I smiled for the first time since the rain started.

"How far down?" Heidi asked in a faint voice.

"Not far. Less than a 'ive minute walk." Kieran took her hand, helping her down and kept her close. "Let's go. You'll feel loads better when you see it."

Lucky girl. For a moment I wished I'd picked the end near the tunnels instead of the one furthest away. *Dummy!* I scolded myself. Now wasn't the time to be jealous of Heidi getting help from Kieran. We had more pressing issues. Like surviving the night!

We waded through the muck in a single-file chain. Whenever I slipped, I grabbed hold of Brent for balance, who walked in front of me. How we managed to walk the route in the darkness, without anyone falling, was beyond me.

It took only minutes, but felt like an hour as we inched our way, finally reaching two steel doors.

Seth grabbed the large, heavy-looking handle and pulled hard. The old door groaned when it finally gave way, as if it didn't want to let us in. I was right about going for the cars. *Could this be another mistake?* I shivered at the crazy thought, but followed the others inside.

Just as I stepped through the doorway, a flash of lightning erupted, illuminating the room, exposing its brilliant white, round shape. Huge concrete pads with towering steel poles reached high into the air. Maybe the poles were once measuring markers or something. *Hopefully not for uranium or radium. That stuff's wicked radioactive.* I'd have asked Heidi, our little photographic memory gal, but I had no intention of trying to scare her any more.

The fifty-foot poles stretched from floor to ceiling. The translucent dome arched like a sunroof above us.

Another zigzagged ember flashed, this one lasting longer. A crackle and boom followed, making me jump inside the circular space. Heidi cried out and buried her head between her knees. Kieran paced along the outside of the room, his fingers running along the perimeter. "The walls have some kind of dust covering them."

The room suddenly went black as tar. A moment later, a loud clap sounded above us. *Crack!* The poles shook against the angry thunder. I closed my eyes, wishing I was anywhere in the world but here. In one of the cars!

Bang!

"What was that?" Heidi screamed.

I covered my ears. If possible, I'd have jumped out of my skin.

"Sorry," said Seth. "The door's heavy. It slipped from my hand."

A piercing howl whistled over our heads. This room was hell on earth.

"'Tis nothing, everyone." Kieran clapped his hands to get the dust off. "Just wind catching through the dome."

We stood back to back in the middle of the room. Brent grabbed mine and Heidi's hands, pulling us down to sit beside him. The others dropped as well. *At least the floor's dry.*

I shoved my hands deep into the pockets of my black vest. My left hand squeezed around a familiar, rectangular object. "Guys! I forgot to hand my phone in when we got to the field." I pulled it out and flipped it open. Its light illuminated the wall in front of me into a blue hue.

"You had it the whole time?" Rylee shook her head.

"It doesn't matter. I can't get any reception here." I held it above my head, aiming in several different directions. "I'll try texting my dad and a couple of people from class. Maybe a message'll go through as it roams." With shaking fingers, I sent the SOS message out to everyone on my BBM list.

"It looks like we're gonna be here for a while," Seth said. "Anyone got anything to say, or any deep, dark secrets they want to tell?"

Rylee coughed. "Yeah, I'm a serial rapist 'n been living undercover in Elliot Lake, pretending to be a female high school student. I'm actually a six-foot male who climbs into this body every day and acts as if –"

"Shut up!" Heidi and I shouted at the same time.

A gust howled outside. The metal pillars creaked and groaned in protest. They were probably holding the sunroof cover in place. I shifted closer to Brent, who put his arm around my shoulders in a brotherly fashion. It helped, a little. The wind's howl switched to a high-pitched shriek, and lightning flickered, building to constant streaks above the dome.

"With how long the bloody lightning lasts, it's like someone's playing with the light switch." On my right, Kieran hunched forward, hugging his knees, his wet shoes and socks beside him on the concrete.

A massive loud boom of thunder rumbled above us, shaking the room. An eerie creaking noise made me glance up momentarily. Then I ducked my head as fast as I could as dust and particles fell from the ceiling, pinging the ground around us. *Could the dome collapse on us?* I grabbed my phone, but there was still no signal. My heart pounded. *I don't want to die here.* Not in this place. Would anybody even find our bodies?

"Everyone all right?" Seth crawled forward and picked something off the ground. "Anyone get hit by a bolt?" Everyone mumbled an okay, and unconsciously we edged our backs closer together. He chuckled. "I think Mother Nature's chasing us down tonight."

No one replied.

Hail joined the humungous raindrops, which pelted the sunroof. Another blast of air whistled by. The sky was lit up like fireworks at Disneyland.

"Amaz—" Brent started.

An awful cracking sound split the air, cutting him off. Terrified, I couldn't stop myself from looking up. The flippin' sunroof shifted and had ripped away from the pillars!

Metal, plastic, and fragments of who knows what showered down. Something hard hit my shoulder. It was probably a tiny screw, but felt like a boulder. I threw my hands over my head and prayed this was just a bad dream. *A nightmare more like.*

"Holy shit!"

I had no idea who said it and didn't care. I just didn't want to die.

Only rain and hail seemed to be falling and swirling into the tower room now. Cautiously, I glanced back up at the dome top.

It wobbled and then hung as if pausing. *Dramatically pausing.* Then it teetered as it fell to rest against a single pillar. *We're so dead.*

I barely blinked when another monstrously strong blast of wind took the entire dome-roof off. It disappeared into the dark night sky.

"Bollocks! Did you just see that?" Kieran jumped to his feet and ran to a pillar, wrapping his arms around it. We watched in shocked silence, letting the hail and rain bombard us.

Lightning illuminated the room again and the rain poured down in sheets.

Seth went to the door. "I can't get the door open."

"Grab a column." Kieran's accented voice carried above the storm. "They're not going anywhere." He pointed to the other poles, one for each of us. "It'll keep you dry. The edge of the ceiling is hangin' far enough over to block the rain. Yer gettin' soaked."

"This sucks," I muttered, jumping up and dashing to the pillar beside Kieran's. I stepped onto the concrete slab, hugged the pole, and shifted toward the wall. *The Scotsman's right.* The small overhang of the remains of the ceiling sheltered me from the pounding rain. I had to hold tight to stop from falling off the thinner side of the slab, but it beat getting soaking wet.

Heidi, Brent, Seth, and Rylee scrambled to the other four pillars. The storm continued to beat down, like it never planned on stopping.

I watched in horror as a bolt discharged through the clouds and shot directly down through the gap. The zigzag light charged down and danced in the place we'd been sitting moments before.

Electric veins reached out to lick the walls and skip around. I closed my eyes, unable to move, too terrified to even think. What a choice – we couldn't let go of the pillars or keep holding on. I could feel the energy and heat in the room, positive we were all going to fry. *Mom, Dad, I love you. I hope you know...*

The hair on my neck and arms stood on end. Actually, every hair follicle felt raised on my skin. A weird smell filled the air. I couldn't place it or correlate it to anything. I thought I could taste the chalky dust. I swallowed to cleanse my tongue and then snorted to try to clear my nose.

The static noise lasted forever. I kept my eyes squeezed tight, too scared to look or breathe. I waited for death, or something close to it.

"Holy shit! Did you see what just happened?"

I tentatively opened one eye, wondering why death sounded so feminine.

The sparks had disappeared, but I swore I could still hear the noise the lightning strike had made so close to us. And the static. It muted when the thunder pounded, and I shook as the noise resonated inside my chest and head.

Death spoke again, sounding a helluva lot like Rylee shouting. Startled, I looked around to find her.

She stood, still hugging her pillar, but her head was thrown back and she was, of all things, laughing. "No one's going to believe this!

I can't believe it." Her voice carried over the storm, making it easy to decipher her words. She began laughing hysterically. "You guys look like Smurfs. You're all blue."

Chapter 3

We glowed. In the weak light, our skin had a tinge of blue. I wiped the back of my hand on my thighs, wondering if the blue would come off. My jeans had the same glowing color so I wasn't surprised it didn't help. "We'd better not be covered in flippin' uranium. We'll be dust, or dead, by morning." I started slapping my legs to get the powder off.

"It's not uranium. The mine's been closed for over twenty years," Rylee said.

"Radioactive particles stay this way for decades," Heidi said.

"Ahhh... Everyone's turning back to normal, no more blue." Rylee said, clearly disappointed, and almost slipping off her pillar. "We're fading."

I couldn't believe she actually was bummed.

"It's incredible none of us got hit," Seth said. "My ears are still ringing from the crackling noise." He sniffed and rubbed his nose. "It stinks in here."

"Do you think the lightning might come in here again?" Heidi shouted, furthest away from me. "Maybe we should try to head back to the tunnel."

"Wait. Listen," Kieran said.

I cocked an ear, willing the sizzling sound echoing in my head to disappear. Everyone stood so still, I could hear everything. *What's Kieran trying to show us?*

"The storm's moving on." He pointed toward the sky. "The lightning and thunder are 'bout six seconds apart now. The storm's

moving west. I betchya the rain's gonna start letting up as well."
His accent made his words sound like a story.

Nobody moved or spoke. It felt like ages, but my watch showed
about two minutes later the rain did lessen. Drops became smaller,
turning into a light drizzle and then stopping completely. The
wind gave a couple of half-hearted howls but then quieted as well.
The dark clouds covering the night sky followed the storm, and
before long, stars and half the moon peeked its way through the
shattered dome.

"It's kinda beautiful." *I can't believe we're alive.* I stepped off the
concrete slab and with hesitant steps, made my way to the middle of
the room. Staring up at the sky, I could hear muffled thuds as the
others followed my lead and jumped off their slabs.

"Freaky. The sky looks as though nothing ever happened." Brent
snapped his fingers. "Hey, is your phone working now, Zoe?"

I pulled it out of my pocket and flipped it open. The roaming
dotted line disappeared and "message sent" flashed on my screen
over and over again as the SOS I'd written earlier finally went out.
"Yeah, the storm must've screwed everything up. I hope it doesn't
come back." I dropped my shoulders and let out a breath I didn't
know I'd been holding. "Can we please get out of here now?" *I just
want to go home.*

Seth splashed his way across the muddy floor toward the doors.
He grunted as he pushed, throwing his shoulder into it. "Door's
stuck." He pulled the handle really hard and the thing ripped right
off the door. He tossed it on the ground and tried pushing against
the door and then moved to the other door, but to no avail. Brent
and Kieran hurried over, trying to help. Panic filled my chest.

Punching the steel, Brent groaned. "Looks like we'll be waiting
here 'til someone answers one of Zoe's texts." He crossed his arms
and shrugged.

"You're jokin'!" I shook my head. "We're trapped, *again?*"

"Just slightly detained," Seth glared at the door and then threw his hands in the air. "It's no big deal. The storm's over now."

"We're probably in its eye." *Let's go, guys. Come on!*

"You girls wanna do some wrestling? We'll watch." Brent clapped his hands and rubbed them together. He gave a good-natured leer. "Now that the skies are clear, it looks like your standing in a mud ring with white on the outside. Just need the ropes."

I stifled a groan. Music-man needed to shut his vocal chords. However, he was right about the white-thing. Still standing in the middle of the round room, I swung around and stared. *Freaky. Really freaky.* "It does seem kinda bright in here." Even without the lightning or key flashlight. *What's going on?*

"Like someone's switched the lights on," Seth said.

"But at a low wattage. 'Pears like the walls are ablaze," added Kieran.

"Ablaze?" Seth laughed. "That a British term or something?"

Kieran smiled, but his lips stayed tight together. I felt his frustration and wished Seth stood within reach so I could swat the back of his head.

Aside from the large puddle of mud in the middle, everything seemed white in color, like a coloring page that hadn't been filled in yet. The walls were stark and pale. Staring at them, I followed the pattern the cracked lines between the bricks made. They seemed unusually bright, almost like they, too, glowed in the dark. I checked the cement slabs we'd been standing on. Even with mud splattered on them, they were white instead of grey. Of fallen particles that had showered down on us, the nuts, bolts and other metal bits were white.

Heidi shivered. "This room's weird. Actually the whole place is creepy. Zoe's always moaning about how she hates this place. Now I totally get it." She hugged herself. "Sorry to be the perpetual wimp, but I'd prefer to get out of here than spend the night. Zoe, can you try your cell again?" Like her hands, her voice trembled slightly.

"Sure." *I don't plan on sleeping here either.* Flipping my cell phone open, I saw there had been two replies to my SOS, and both thought I'd been joking. "I'm not sure it'll work, but I'll try again." I dialed dad's number.

"Hu-llo?" His voice came across the line low and tired.

"Dad? It's me. We're stranded in the mine. Help!" *Shoot! He's so gonna freak.* I lowered my voice to a normal level and checked my watch. *Just after two a.m.* "Sorry. Were you sleeping?"

"What's wrong?" He sounded instantly awake. "Where are you? Did you say the mine?"

His bed creaked in the background and I knew he'd sat up, probably already shoving his feet into the Crocs he kept by the bed. Having a doctor for a father, worries tended to get blown out of proportion. One of the reasons he and mom split.

"I'm not hurt. Relax." I exhaled a slow breath and fought to control my voice. "But we're in a bit of a bind. The gang all went to the high school kickoff tonight and a storm blew in. We went for cover in the old uranium mine and we're... kinda stuck." He may be the calmest doctor on the continent, but when it came to his only daughter, he turned into the biggest worrywart. I was at mom's this weekend so he would assume I'd be home sleeping in my bed. He was probably having a coronary right now.

"I'm on my way. Have you called nine-one-one?" My pause had him talking again. "Have you tried *anyone* else?"

I knew what was coming.

"Come on, Zoezey."

I sighed. "No, I haven't called mom. I'm sleeping at Rylee's tonight." I could hear him getting dressed and imagined him holding the phone with his chin against his shoulder, throwing on jeans and a sweatshirt. He was probably leaning over to grab his doctor's bag, dark hair falling in his face. "My cell just started working."

"I'll call Jim." Seth's dad, Jim, was a fireman with a huge, muscular body. He could probably remove the fallen tree with his bare hands and then tear down the mine doors with his pinkie finger.

"You'd better call Brent's dad and the rest of the gang's dads. I'm not sure my phone will keep working. I don't even know if the storm's going to start up again. It's all... all..." I swallowed trying not to cry. My throat tightened and burned.

"I'm coming, sweetie," he said, car keys jingling in the background. "I'll call nine-one-one and everyone I need to. Keep your cell close."

"Please hurry." I shut the phone and waved it at my friends, not sure I could speak. "Help's on the way."

"Hopefully Seth's dad is driving the ladder truck over here to rescue us right now," Heidi said.

"I'm sure he's on his way." Seth came and put his arm around Heidi.

"We're all okay and going to get outta here very soon." Brent came and stood by me.

The scepticism of the past few hours eased. Exhaustion seeped into my core. I dropped onto one of the concrete slabs. The others followed my lead. There we sat, and waited. And waited. Bored, we needed someone to talk about something... *anything* to keep our minds off the fact we were still trapped. *Small talk.* "Kieran, where's your new place?"

He ran a hand through his thick, brown hair. "Me granddad owned the wooden cabin thingy near the roundabout—sorry, I mean the four-way stop. He left it to me dad in 'is will."

Rylee, sitting near him, rested a hand on his shoulder. "Sorry to hear you lost your grandfather."

"It was like three years ago. Guess me dad 'n him were not that close. Plus, he was a miserable ol' bugger." Kieran laughed, and all three females turned toward the husky sound. He didn't seem to notice. "Me dad decided to up 'n come here for the year. I wasn't too keen, but he tends to not give a toss to what I think." He shrugged and shot a glance in my direction.

I couldn't read his face. His accent was sexy, even when he sounded ticked off at his dad. With his Sean Connery voice, I had to listen closely to what he said. It might be fun having a new guy in the group. Senior year just got a lot more interesting.

"What'd your mom think about having to come to Canada?" Rylee asked.

"Me mum passed away a few years back. It's just me dad now."

Rylee's hands flew to her face and her eyes grew big. She patted his arm. "Sorry. I sometimes open my mouth when I shouldn't."

Seth smirked. "Sometimes? I think you like puttin' your foot in your mouth."

"Shut up!" Rylee laughed and gave Seth, who sat on her other side, a shove. "At least my mother doesn't bake cookies in the shape of NHL teams for me."

"Hey! I like Seth's mom's cookies," Heidi suddenly piped up. "I'm hoping she sent some with you tonight and you left them in the truck." Poor Heidi, skinny as a toothpick and always hungry.

"Speaking of food, I'm starving!" Seth grabbed his stomach.

I groaned, trying to swallow against dryness in my mouth. "I'm kinda thirsty."

"Me too." Heidi said. "Hungry, thirsty, and soaking."

"Hopefully someone arrives soon," Brent said. "I'm wiped." Everyone must've felt the same as we all grew quiet and waited.

Dad sent a text to let us know the firefighters were working on removing the large fallen tree at the entrance to the mine. We could hear muffled noise from the dome. He sent another text forty minutes later asking where we were.

It took almost an hour for the search and rescue team to find us.

When voices on the other side of the locked door greeted us, we hollered. The room had grown darker as the moon shifted.

The saw-cutters and drills had me covering my ears from the screeching noise. The loud banging from some heavy metal thing slamming against the door seemed to last forever. It broke my heart when I heard one of the firefighters say they'd have to try the other door.

"Anyone 'ver watch Fireman Sam?" Kieran asked loudly, trying to be heard over the noise. "Tom Thomas could fly his little helicopter and lift us out of here with a rope. Seems yer firefighters could use ol' Sam."

"Huh?" Seth chuckled. "That was my favourite show when I was a kid. My dad had an uncle from England send DVDs over." He laughed harder. Kieran joined in.

"You guys are messed up!" I tried frowning but couldn't stop the smile. *Could this night get any crazier?*

The firefighters finally broke down the other door. Their flashlights were so bright, they had all of us holding our hands out to covering our eyes.

Rylee stood closest to the door and yelped when the light hit her eyes. "Turn that thing off, please!" She staggered like she'd been hit. Seth grabbed her arm to steady her.

One fireman swept his torch over the walls. I nudged Kieran and pointed. "They're black." I kept my voice low.

"Wha'?" he said.

"The walls, they're black now. Weren't they sorta glowing in the dark before?" I continued to whisper.

He blinked, and scratched his left temple. "Yeah, 'tis weird. Maybe it was the moon."

Four more firefighters filed through the door, one of them Seth's dad. Jim's boisterous voice shouted commands and had us walking out single file, holding onto a rope with a fireman between each of us. We laughed at the bright yellow rope, but Jim insisted we use the buddy system so no one would be left behind.

Ten minutes later we stood on the wet grass among flashing cop cars, fire trucks, and the local TV crew. *Only in a small town, the freakin' media's got nothing more exciting to cover?* I found my dad a split second before he noticed me. He stood, hands in his back pockets of his jeans, doctor bag hanging over his shoulder and his right foot tapping.

He ran over and squeezed me tight. "Everyone okay?" He motioned to Jim and walked to get his medical bag where he'd dropped it when he'd dashed over. "Let's get all of you to the ambulance. Check and see if you're all okay."

A policeman stepped forward. "Your folks have been notified," he paused when he reached Kieran, "except yours, young man. We didn't realize there were six of you." He handed Kieran the cell from his chest pocket. "Here. Call your folks."

Kieran pushed the phone back at the officer. "Thanks, but I'll let me Dad know in the morning. No sense in waking 'im if everything's all right."

Poor guy. He's embarrassed by the officer's concern. I inhaled a deep breath, about to say something. The air smelled of wet earth. It felt like mud clogged in my throat. I gagged and began coughing.

Dad rushed back to my side and pounded my back. "You okay?"

Holy smokes. You don't need to shout, Dad. I bent forward and raised a hand. "I'm... okay..." I tried to clear my air passage. "A bug must've been... trying to... suffocate me." I swallowed and took shallow breaths. "Honest, I'm fine." *Please don't embarrass me.*

"I'll get you home soon, kiddo." Dad put his arm around my shoulder when I straightened. "Let me just check the others and we'll go. My car's parked beside the first ambulance."

I rested my head on his chest, suddenly exhausted. "The Bug's parked somewhere in the field."

"We'll get it in the morning."

Seth spoke from behind. "I'll take it back to my place. Kieran can drive my truck."

"Thanks." I lifted my head. It felt so heavy.

Rylee's folks had come and, to my surprise, Heidi's mom was here on her own. It made me wish mom were here, but the feeling quickly evaporated.

I tried to focus on my friends, but my eyes rolled from sudden exhaustion. I tried blinking several times to refocus but gave up. Tapping Dad's shoulder, I asked, "Is it okay if I wait in your car?"

He bent down to grab something out of his medical bag. "Let me check you once more –"

"Dad! I'm fine." I winced at the harshness in my tone, and lowered my voice. "Nothing happened in the mine. We just got stuck in that stupid room." I didn't want to be here another minute. The ambulances' flashing red lights bounced off the front of the mine. The entrance looked like a face laughing at us with horrible beady red eyes. I shuddered and mumbled, "So... tired... just gonna lie down... in the car." I walked to his Beemer, grabbing a blanket and bottle of water from the back of the ambulance as I passed. I crawled into the backseat and took a swig from the bottle. The refreshing liquid never tasted so delicious. My body collapsed across the seats, my arms pulling the blanket over my head. Everything sounded so loud outside.

I woke groggy sometime later. It took me a moment to remember what happened. *Ugh! What a lousy night.* The cut-off of the engine told me we were in Dad's driveway. He cleared his throat and I heard him move to reach over to the passenger seat, probably grabbing his bag. When he opened the door, the irritating beeping sounded to remind him to take the keys from the ignition.

Reaching for the handle, I pulled myself up and crept outside. The cool air made me shiver. I hugged myself and groggily made my way to Dad's front door. A figure stood silhouetted in the light on the porch. I groaned, wishing I had the ability to disappear, or better yet, some supernatural power to make my mom disappear.

Mom began shouting at Dad, oblivious to the late hour. "You bastard! Why didn't you call me sooner?" She stoped her foot. "She could've been seriously hurt."

Dad said nothing. He put his arm around my shoulders and helped me inside the house and whispered to me, "She's just worried about you." Once we were through the front door, he turned back to corral my unbelievably loud mother. She wouldn't shut up.

"She could've drowned, or been hit by lightning or—"

"Bev," Dad said, using his doctor-talking-to-the-patient voice, "why not come inside and I'll make you a cup of coffee. You must be cold from waiting." Good ol' Dad, making her think it was in *her* best interest to come in.

They came inside, Dad holding the door for my stomping mother. She paused in front of me and began touching and patting me everywhere.

"Are you hurt?" *Pat, pat, pat.*

"No, Mom. Stop. Nothing's broken. Dad's already checked me out. I'm fine."

"We should take you to the hospital. Who knows what rodents are living in that mine."

I stepped out of her reach. "I'm all right." I glanced at Dad for help.

He smiled and shrugged, as if saying "what can you do?" He squeezed my shoulder. "Let's talk over a cup of coffee, Bev."

Mom glared at him. "You're right we're going to talk." She stormed into the kitchen.

Dad gave me a sympathetic smile. "I'll calm her down. Why don't you go on and clean up." He pulled at a strand of my hair, and dried dirt fell to the floor.

That's why I loved him. He got me without having to explain things sometimes. "Thanks. I'm gonna jump in the shower. I stink."

"—and I think there's more mud on you than most pigs." He hugged me tight, pulling away when my mother called out she couldn't work the coffee machine. I smiled. Dad had one of those automatic coffeemakers. It made lattes, hot chocolates, the works. Actually, a drink sounded really good.

He must have seen my face. "I'll make something hot and soothing for you to drink, and put it in your room." He kissed my forehead. "Goodnight, sweetie. I'll see you in morning." He headed down the hall to the kitchen.

I shook my head when Mom started in on Dad. She always did that. Whenever she couldn't handle a situation, she blamed it on him. She didn't mean to, but it was her way of dealing with crap. Plus tonight she talked so bloomin' loud, it grated on my ears. She just didn't know how to handle intense situations. *If she'd just leaned on Dad instead of blaming him, maybe...* I forced the thought out of my head. I loved my mom and she was great. She just had a tendency to overreact. Usually it wasn't a big deal, but tonight, I just couldn't handle it.

I headed to the room Dad had set up for me five years ago when he'd bought the house shortly after their separation. I lived with Mom but slept here as much as I could. I grabbed a pair of cotton PJ bottoms with a tank top and headed downstairs. Dad had this awesome huge double shower installed down there.

Turning both jets on high, I stripped down and stepped in. The hot water pounded on my back and top of my head. It felt awesome. The power of the jets drowned out my parents' voices. A headache began creeping up the back of my neck and spreading like a vice around my head. I washed my mud-caked legs and scrubbed the dirt out of my hair. If my head didn't hurt so badly, I'd have enjoyed the shower longer. All I wanted to do was crawl into bed and vanish for the next hundred hours. I never got migraines and this felt debilitating.

I dressed and paused at the kitchen entrance. Dad had calmed Mom down. They each sat on a barstool, having a glass of wine. Mom was laughing at something Dad said, her slender fingers resting on his bicep.

She stood when she saw me and came over to give me a hug. "Glad you're okay." She kissed my forehead. "Ready to go?"

"I-I...uh..." I stood there in PJs and she wanted to take me home? Some people were actually getting up at this time to go to work!

"Bev." Dad rested his hand on her shoulder. "Why not let Zoezey sleep here. It's almost morning, and she's exhausted."

Her brows creased together and she opened her mouth.

"Mom," I interrupted, stopping any chance of her speaking. "My head's killin'. I'm gonna lie down. You finish your wine. If I'm still awake when you're done, I'll come back with you."

She nodded, and from behind her shoulder, Dad winked at me.

"G'night." I turned and headed upstairs, not waiting for their wishes or kisses. I shuffled to my bedroom, barely able to keep my eyes open from the pounding in my head. I really had a new sympathy for migraine sufferers. If I could fall asleep before it hit full-on, I'd avoid the worst of it. I stumbled into bed, shoving the pillow over my ears to drown out my parents. They were so hot and cold, sometimes I felt like the adult.

Noises all around screamed deep into my ear canals. There was no escape into darkness, just the shards and fracturing across the inside of my eyelids. Too exhausted to fight, I lay there tortured, unable to move.

Chapter 4

Ka-poosh!... Ka-poosh... Kapoosh!

I groaned and threw the duvet over my face. When that didn't deafen the jackhammer outside, I grabbed the pillow and stuffed it over my head. *It's freakin' Sunday morning and Dad's idiot neighbour has to rip the concrete out of his driveway NOW?*

Ka-poosh!

Bolting upright, I chucked the pillow at the closet. The noise continued to echo in my ears and ricochet inside my head. I glanced at the nightstand, swearing I'd just heard the click of the numbers changing. *Impossible. Seeing as it's freakin' digital.*

Six a.m., right on the button.

Rubbing my eyes, I checked again. Yeah, I'd read it correctly. I banged my head against the pillow. Except it wasn't there. It lay on the floor by my closet.

Three hours of sleep. *Seriously?*

I punched the mattress and pushed myself out of bed. I jerked back, startled when an echo from the bed's springs squealed against my eardrums. Stomping to the window, I flipped open Dad's expensive California shutters. The street below lay void of life. The neighbour didn't have a hard hat crew jacking up the concrete; only his Lexus sat in the driveway. Dad lived in the rich side of town where all the professional doctors, lawyers, and whoever were all still in bed this morning. Only a stupid fly with an annoying buzz banged into the glass a few times before finally taking off.

Still, the *Ka-poosh* noise didn't stop. I turned from the window and slumped against the wall. I shut my eyes tight as more sounds crashed against my eardrums—my father snoring... a dog barking... the fridge running... a screen door slamming...

My eyes shot open. *Dad's asleep so why would the back door be closing?* My brows mashed together. *Wait. He doesn't have a screen door.* It was one of those metal doors with the fancy rainbow glass. *Maybe the neighbors?*

Heart pounding against my ribs, each rapid beat reverberated inside my skull, like church bells. My head hurt like hell. Last night's thunderstorm fiasco came flooding back. The creepy mine, the weird blue skin, Mom and Dad's fight, and the exhaustion.

Too tired to notice pretty much anything. Maybe I'd caught a cold. *Ear infection?* I pressed my fingers against the bridge of my nose. No pressure or congestion. *I feel good, like I've slept ten hours instead of three.* I snorted but stopped instantly, the noise seemed to scream into my hearing canal. *Well, my body feels rested. My head feels like a train wreck between the ears.* I plugged my ears.

Ka-poosh!

I marched out of the room, determined to find whoever was responsible for the annoying sound. I trudged through Dad's entire backsplit, nearly falling down when I got to the bottom of the basement stairs. The *ka-poosh* noise became clearer. I yanked the bathroom door open, not giving a crap who might be inside. About to yell, my voice froze in my throat.

No drill or jackhammer here either, but the noise was deafening. Plugging my ears again, I walked to the shower. "Holy crap." I jumped back, surprised that even my voice sounded way too loud to my poor ears. The stall stood vacant, but the faucet hadn't been completely shut off. Water dripped from the showerhead, making the distinctive *ka-poosh* sound.

How in the world did I hear that tiny drip from upstairs in my bed? *How'd it wake me up?* As I realized the sound, it blended in with the other noises of the house. Distinct, but everything else I heard seemed to be fighting for attention inside my head. I could even hear Dad snoring three floors up. *I'm like a bloody animal. If someone blows one those dog whistles I'll probably hear it and start howling.*

Cranking the faucet tight, my thoughts drifted back to the mine. I never planned on stepping foot inside there again... ever. *Earwax.* I grabbed two Q-tips and tried clearing my ears out. It sounded like a river rushing though my head. The tips came away barely dirty. *What the—?*

I pushed the rising panic aside and tossed the tips in the garbage can. I tugged at my ear lobes as I made my way up the stairs. I needed some Advil and breakfast. Hopefully, that would clear my headache and my hypersensitive ears.

Once inside the slightly clinical-feeling, chrome-filled kitchen, I popped waffles into the toaster. After setting my plate as quietly as I could on the little breakfast bar in the middle of the room, I swung open the fridge to grab syrup. I squawked when a high-pitched *urrrr* sound grated in the air. Grimacing, I whirled around to trail the sound. *Toaster.* There must've been some kind of short in it. I jerked the cord from the wall, my shoulders instantly relaxing. I hadn't even noticed they'd tensed up.

I stared at my white knuckles gripping the edge of the counter. *Something's so wrong.* I could tune into every sound in the house... and I mean all of it, on every floor, and outside. *Focus, Zoe. You can control this. You tune Mom and Dad out all the time.*

I shut my eyes, attempting to squash the building panic inside. Except closing my eyes only enhanced my hearing into supersonic radars. I couldn't control it. My eyelids popped up at a sudden thought. *No human can possibly hear with such clarity without help.*

My chest swelled and stiffened, ready to explode. The tightness crept up my throat. I flipped around, leaning against the counter and stared at everything. The dishwasher, the fridge, the clock on the stove, the lights above me, a pounding creak near the stairs. Each time my eyes settled on something, my hearing tuned into a new sound. *All the normal things in my life are now enemies invading my head.*

"Crap, crap, crap," I whispered, the heels of my hands covered my eyes and my fingernails scratched into my scalp. The scraping on my skin sounded like nails on a chalkboard. I shuddered. Even my barely audible cry sounded like wailing to me.

"What's going on, Zoe?"

I nearly hit the ceiling from Dad's groggy voice. He stood at the kitchen doorway in hospital scrubs and a creased white tee shirt. *Get outta here. Fake a yawn, go back to bed. Avoid doctor dad.* His creamed coffee-colored hair had major bed-head on the left side. He walked to the fridge and pulled out a container of OJ, drinking straight from the jug.

As I stared at his large, bare feet, each gulp he swallowed bounced inside my ear canals. His heart beat between each swallow—*glug-thump-glug-thump.* I swore if I concentrated hard enough, I'd hear the blood rushing through his veins.

He put the juice back in the fridge, and shut the door with his heel as he turned to watch me. The concern on his face comforted me. I relaxed my shoulders, but felt like I couldn't breathe.

"You look like you're in pain." He placed a cool hand on my forehead, and then the back of my neck. "You're a bit warm."

I stepped back, out of his reach. "I'm all right." I took a slow, shallow breath in and out. "Just a bit of a headache." I didn't want him to worry... yet.

Too late. He disappeared from the kitchen for a moment, and I heard him grab his medical bag from the chair near the front door. *Crap! I don't need this right now. I just want to be on my own... figure this out.* He reappeared and dropped the bag on the counter.

I flinched at the loud sound each clasp made when he clipped the bag open.

"I want to do some blood work on you. Who knows what got into your system at that old mine." He pulled out a needle and a couple of vials. "Sit." He pointed to one of the chairs at the breakfast nook along the wall. "I'm heading into the office for an hour."

Not in the mood to argue, I dropped into a chair and grimaced as it creaked. *Slow movements, quiet as possible.* How could I have forgotten that already?

I swear I heard my tendons snap as I straightened my arm. Dad tied a tourniquet around my bicep.

"Make a fist."

"I know the drill, Dad. I've done this before." *Wow, we're having a shouting match and he doesn't even know it.*

"Just making sure." He swiped the area with an alcohol swab.

I closed my eyes, not wanting to see the needle go into my flesh. The sharp pinch was enough for me. A unique buzzing filled my ears, and when the needle pricked my skin and entered my vein, I flinched. I picked up a weird sucking sound, like a vacuum and then the sound of my blood whooshing into the vial. It took everything within me not to pull away or try to cover my ears with my free arm. *Act normal.* Three vials filled; each click and popping sound discrete to my oversensitive ears.

I stared at the vials and caught my Dad's heart rate switching to a faster pace. The blood inside had a purple tinge to it. Was that normal?

"There, kiddo. All done." Dad pressed a cotton ball and bandage on my arm. He stood and put the blood into a mini-centrifuge container he kept in the bag. "I'm going to jump in the shower, and then head out."

"Do you think..." I swallowed, afraid to finish my thought, "something...might be off?"

He hugged me. "No. I just want to double check. I have no idea if there's still radium in the mine. There might be uranium in there and if you kids inhaled any..." He sighed and pulled away. "Everything's fine. I just prefer to err on the side of caution."

I nodded but said nothing. I'd heard the change in his heart rate again and knew he was either lying or scared. So was I.

Dad squeezed my shoulder and headed back to his room. As I watched his retreating figure, I wondered why he'd never dated. He had a great job, he was handsome and fit. Women threw themselves at him all the time when we went out or when I visited him at his office. Mom had done a number on him. She'd broken his heart beyond repair. *Great. Now I'm all sentimental like I'm about to die.*

The pulsing water from Dad's shower broke me out of my wandering thoughts. With my weird super-hearing, I listened to him step in and the water hit his body. *Gross* I didn't need to listen to his morning routine.

Running for the safety of my bedroom, I dove into bed, thrust my head under the pillow and pulled the covers over. Dad's electric razor sounded like a lawnmower, even when I tried muffling the sound.

A part of me tried to convince the rest of myself this could be something really cool. *Maybe, but it's a nightmare at the same time.*

What about the others? Had the same thing happened to them?

I crawled out from under the sheets and grabbed my Blackberry. Rylee and Heidi were first on my BBM list.

I sent them both a message: *U ok? Let's meet 2nite.*

Dropping back onto the bed I shut my eyes tight and counted the loud echo of my heartbeats. It was easy to pick out the *dub-lub* sound my heart made as blood poured through its chambers. I tried to block out the horrible thoughts.

It was no use.

My cell lit up and its buzzing sounded like a bee's nest.

Rylee replied: *WTH? I got a massive migraine + can't stop crying.*

Chapter 5

Brent

Somehow the sun figured out a way to sneak through my blinds and stab my pillow. At first it didn't bother me. Half awake, the guitar dream felt too good to be true. *Aw! Why couldn't it be real?* When my left hand started tingling, I rolled over. Sunshine clawed its way through my closed eyelids so I rolled over and moved my head into the shade. Ten minutes later the blinding light zapped me again.

Irritated, I flipped onto my back and grabbed the remote on the nightstand. Now my right hand prickled. I must've slept on a nerve or something. I pressed the power button and the fifty-inch flat screen hanging on my wall flickered to life. Much Music had some greaty-eighties videos playing and the satellite info on the top right corner showed just after eleven.

Eyes still fuzzy from sleeping, I got up and staggered into my bathroom to take a leak. Returning to the bedroom, I caught sight of my open guitar case and ran my fingers over the wood of the Hagstrom. A weird flash fogged my vision – I stumbled and caught the back of the chair before I wiped out.

"Weird." *Could I still be dreaming? Nah...* I bent down, checking my newest baby. If she'd gotten ruined last night outside the mine... didn't even want to imagine. Nate bitched and complained the entire time in Europe about her bulkiness and me lugging her everywhere we went, but I didn't give a toss. It probably cost me half my soul to buy, but the Hagstrom was worth every penny.

The case had water damage on the base, but hey, that's what they're for. It's not like I couldn't get a new one. Finally arriving home in my room last night, I'd immediately opened it, paranoid it'd gotten wet. Then I'd dropped on my bed, too exhausted to get up, check it, or close the case.

The guitar begged me to stroke her. I slid my thumb across the strings, enjoying the sensation it brought. I strummed a few chords and wrapped my fingers around her neck. No rush, I could play a bit before heading downstairs.

The fingers on both hands vibrated against the Maplewood fretboard and the copper-bound steel strings. I pulled back. A tingling sensation zinged from the tips of my fingers up my length of my arm. Staring at my hand, I blinked. Brushing off the feeling, I leaned forward to play again.

"What the—" Again, freaky tremors bounced against my hand and my vision distorted. I tried to focus by squinting, but a shadowy silhouette appeared before me playing my guitar. The guy in the Liverpool shop I'd bought her from said she'd come out of a house on Abbey Road. I hadn't believed him, but the blurry guy in my vision kind of looked like a young version of Sir McCartney. *Okay, my totally overactive imagination is getting the best of me. I'm still dreaming.*

Or, Nate was playing tricks on me. Maybe he had some electric trickle wire leading to the guitar. I dropped to the floor in a push-up position, intending to check the wires.

The moment my fingers touched the dark floor, I froze. The hardwood thrummed against my hands, and a clear image of what appeared, suspiciously, flashed in front of my eyes. My folks sat in the brightly sunlit dining room, directly below, having brunch. Dad reading the paper, and Mom checking messages on her iPad.

I stood and staggered backward, rubbing my forehead. Wait a sec—-Nate couldn't have rigged my guitar. He left for UofT last week.

I grabbed a tee shirt and a pair of faded blue jeans. I groaned. *Ah, hell, Rosetta had ironed them – again*. How many times did I have to ask her to take them just out of the dryer? I preferred my pants kinda crinkled. No kid my age ironed his pants. Complaining didn't help. She'd just start ironing my boxer-briefs and leave smiley-face post-it notes. I loved her anyway. She was our housemaid, but part mom at the same time.

Giddy laughter floated up the stairs. Mom reacting to something Dad said. I followed their voices and the smell of fresh cinnamon buns and coffee into the dining area, then shook my head at the moment of déjà vu. *Say what? How could I know?* I gave my head a slight shake. *Nah, it's just their normal routine*. I clenched and unclenched my hands, trying to stop the annoying prickly sensation.

"You're up." Dad folded his paper and leaned back in his chair. He wore a suit – strange for a Saturday. "Surprising. You usually don't show your face till at least noon."

"How're you feeling?" Mom ran a finger back and forth along her pearl necklace.

"Fine, I guess." I shrugged, ignoring Dad's comment. "My head's killing me."

Mom rested a cool hand on the nape of my neck. "You're a bit warm. Do you think I should phone Dr. Taylor and ask him do a house call?"

Dad harrumphed.

"I'm fine, Mom." I leaned over and kissed her cheek smelling sweet perfume against her collar. "I probably just need to eat." I grabbed a croissant, loaded it with ham and cheese, and took a huge bite. Tingling seemed to have finally stopped. I settled into the chair across from my father and nodded at him. Mom wore a fancy outfit. *Both dressed up?* Probably going to one of Dad's functions.

"I've got one of my surveyors coming tomorrow to look at the mine. He'll run a few tests on the uranium. See if there's any trace amounts and make sure the mine's properly closed. That place is a sore spot in this town. I'd like to see it turned into a golf course." He glanced at Mom. "I'm going to check with the city to see if that's possible. It'd be the perfect location and I don't own a course. I'd love to design one." He pulled his iPad out and began making notes.

Keeping my head down, I rolled my eyes. He wants a golf course? Now he thinks he's a designer? No worry his son might be full of toxins or who-knows-the-hell-what?

"Nate called this morning." Mom slipped on her white suit jacket and straightened it. She wiped invisible dirt off the matching white skirt. She always wore white the last day before Labor Day. Said it had to do with some fashion thing.

"What'd he say?" Nate'd be psyched to hear about last night.

"I told him you spent the night in the mine. He wants you to phone him with all the details." Mom turned to Dad. "Time to go, honey. The invitation said three o'clock, and it'll take us an hour to get there."

Dad sighed. He stood and tossed his napkin on the table. "I'd love to have one Sunday with no commitments. What happened to family days?" He pulled his phone out as he followed my mother toward the hallway. "Do you mind driving, dear? I'll make a few phone calls regarding the possibility of the golf course. If I can't do it at the mine, I want to find another location now that I've got it in my head."

Mom looked at me and winked. "One of your dad's business partners invited us to his retirement party. I'm not sure what time we'll be back. It shouldn't be too late." She picked up her purse off the buffet and slipped it over her shoulder. "Rosetta put a chicken on the rotisserie and there's salad in the fridge. Don't forget to call Nate."

"Okeydokey." I stood and followed them to the front entrance. *Their social obligations always seemed to trump any possibility of having a real conversation with them.* "See ya later." I closed the door and stood there a moment with my hand remaining on the door.

Startled, I jerked away but kept my hand on the heavy, oak door. The weird tingling sensation returned, but with a force that spasmed all the way up to my eyeballs. The door was antique, with lead windows high up on the top, but it felt like my fingers had drilled little holes and gave me perfect vision outside... like a window.

I could see my parents walk outside toward the three-car garage. My dad patted my mom's ass, which she reciprocated with a playful shove.

"What the fu—," I mumbled, pulling my hand away. The image disappeared when the pressure of the wood left my fingers. Curious, I raised both hands and tentatively touched the door with the tips of my fingers. The entire yard came into view. The garage door opening, my folks pulling out, disappearing down the drive. *I can see through frickin' doors?*

Weird. But while watching outside, I could also see the door in front of me. It took a bit of focussing, but I figured out how to switch back and forth—inside, then outside, then back inside. Keeping one hand on the door, I turned sideways. Now I could see the dining room table, or anywhere else I looked, and still see outside at will.

I could spy on people – hot girls in particular – or play a killer trick on Seth. The possibilities were endless.

"This is so effing cool!" I shouted to the empty house. No need to swear with no one to hear me. My head pounded. Shouting wasn't a smart idea. Suddenly my brain hurt like a son of a bitch. Even my eyes ached like they had weights on them.

I need my phone. It took everything I had to trudge up the stairs. Lightheaded and dizzy, I clung to the railing and tried to ignore the tingling feeling now spreading to my feet.

Swallowing the bile rising in my throat, I dropped to the floor when I made it past the last step. Crawling toward the stand beside my bed, I grew nauseous from the see-through floor because of my fingers and trying to find my way through my foggy eyes. When I reached my bed, it took everything in me not to hurl.

Still on all fours and my forehead pressed against the floor, I reached on top of the stand and let my hand find my Blackberry. Blowing a hard breath from my lips, I gingerly sat up and leaned against the bed.

Eyes open in slits, I sent Seth and Zoe a text. Zoe and I had been great buds since preschool. Too bad I didn't have the courage to tell her I wouldn't mind being something more. Last night I'd hoped to ask her out. Except she'd been goggling over the new guy, and then the thunderstorm screwed everything up. *At least I have this wicked cool touchy-thing to make up for it.* My thumbs found the keys and I didn't even need to look at the screen.

Meet 2nite. 7pm PHP Have something cool 2 show u

I wanted to try the touch-feely thing outside. *See what happens when I put my hand on the grass.* I pushed myself up and leaned against the bed. It took several deep breaths top stop the room from the spinning. Walking like a drunk bum, I made it past my door and down the hall.

Then my brain decided to spin the house like a tornado. I pressed my fingers against my temple and buried my head into my palms. Another sensation pushed into my conscience – like Dorothy's house in the Wizard of Oz.

I realized what was happening – a second too late.

Chapter 6

Rrrrr...Rrrrrr...

My phone vibrated against my cheek. I must've rolled onto it in my sleep. I'd passed out big time.

I opened my eyes and nearly shit my pants. *Holy crap! What the hell happened?* I lay on the top of the stairs. Well, sort of. My hips and legs were on the landing, but my upper body lay sprawled down on the top two steps. The moments before passing out came flooding back. How I hadn't toppled down the stairs was beyond me.

Slowly I crawled backwards until there were no more steps. *Headache's gone, thank goodness.* Except my body still felt weak and shaky. I crawled back to my room and dropped onto my bed, tossing my phone beside me.

Stretching, I glanced around my room. Five guitars rested peacefully on their stands but my new one still lay on the floor beside the bed. *How irreverent of me.*

A tingling in my toes reminded me of more important things. I leaned to the side and touched the wall. My fingers brought Nate's room into focus, even clearer than before. *Freakin' awesome! I still got it.*

I punched the bed in excitement, rolled off, and stood barefoot on the hardwood floor. An image of the dining room flashed in front of my eyes at the exact moment the bottom of my feet touched. *My feet now have eyes? What's going on with my skin? I gotta figure out how to control this or I'll go crazy.* Distracted, I nearly stepped on my guitar. I caught myself and went to splash cold water on my face.

"Holy shit!" I stared at the reflection in my mirror, towel in hand. My eyebrows hid under my hair, and my mouth hung open. *I'm surprised the vision didn't come from my jaw hitting the floor.* Moving closer, it seemed as if my blue eyes had more specs of brown in them. Or they were just bluer. *Nah... impossible.*

Still gawking, I spread my feet shoulder width apart. After seeing my face in the mirror and the room below, I touched the wall. My freak skill allowed me to see Nate's room, the dining room and my reflection, all at the same time. It took some time, but by shifting my focus slightly by moving my eyes, I figured out how to switch rooms. It made my head spin so I dropped the toilet seat down and sat. I could touch the floor and both walls.

I needed to slow down or I'd throw up. Feet on the floor, I shoved my hands under my armpits and worked on shifting scenes without getting dizzy. Once accomplished, I added one hand, then the other. Soon I could focus on what I wanted to see, and still see the other rooms peripherally, like a computer screen that had different screens which popped up by simply touching them. Pacing in my room, I needed to figure out how to have the ability to see my normal field of sight. I'd either never be able to move or I'd crash into everything if I didn't get it sorted.

Dropping my arms and shaking them, I gave my shoulders a few rolls and started from my feet up again. First one foot I concentrated on the screen views my brain gave me. Sweat broke out on my forehead but I knew I was getting there. The dizziness disappeared as well as the nausea. When I finally added a hand to the wall and manoeuvred around my guitars without banging into anything, I relaxed. *Easy as pie.* Laughter erupted from my throat, and I did a Tiger Woods fist pump, then nicely finished off with two long blasts from the old butt trumpet.

A buzzing stopped my victory dance. My phone slid a few inches on my sheets, trying to get my attention. I picked it up and checked for messages. There were three. Seth said he'd meet up and would stop by Kieran's place to see if he wanted to come. Heidi texted that Zoe had sent her a message and she'd let Rylee know, and they'd be there.

Zoe sent the last one.

⊠ ⊠ **Sorry 4 not replying sooner. Mom's freaking out since I didn't call her when I was at my dad's. I'm walking 2 mom's now and getting the Beatle. C U at PHP. I gotta tell you something.** ⊠⊠

Poor gal, she had no idea how to send a short text. I couldn't help but grin. *I gotta tell you something wayyy cooler.* Unless she had the same thing happen to her. *Something from the mine...*

I replied: *L8er.*

Tossing the phone on the bed, I then bent over and picked up Hagstrom, unable to resist playing it. I settled onto the stool near the fireplace on the far wall and ran my fingers over the strings, playing a few odd chords. I'd always preferred fingers over a pick. Now, the vibrations humming through my fingers were like magic, like I'd never understood the sound until that moment.

I disappeared into the melody as the notes rang out. Nothing else existed. There was only the music. Not like before, so much more... deeper, sensual.

The next time I checked my watch, I stared in surprise. *Two and a half hours gone?* It'd felt like twenty minutes since I'd come to at the top of the stairs. Six o'clock and I still needed to shower before heading out to PHP. Jumping from the stool, I carefully set the guitar on her stand and raced to the bathroom.

The log cabin exterior of Pool Hall Parlour twinkled with year-round with multi-colored Christmas lights. A few old cars in the parking lot, but none looked familiar. Once inside, I checked to see if any of the gang had been dropped off. At home, I'd figured out when I wore socks or sneakers, my feet were unable to get any X-ray vision. It made driving a whole lot easier.

Running my fingers along the wooden walls, I searched the eating and pool table area, even the 'Cowpokes' restroom. I lifted my hand as I passed the 'Cowgals'. There were certain things in life a guy didn't need to see. Nobody was here yet.

Funny, I've been here a million times but everything seems like I'm seeing it for the first time. Way clearer. *Maybe my focus is notched just a little tighter.*

Whoever decorated PHP must've made some taxidermist rich. Stuffed raccoons, beavers, ducks, fish, and deer heads plastered the walls over the pool tables, bar, and video games. A huge black moose loomed over the dart board, a couple of stray darts stuck to him. The one by its nose was mine.

Aside from never wanting to be here on your own with all those beady eyes watching your every move, the place had an awesome atmosphere. It only added to the awesome food they served. Huge burgers which tasted like proper outdoor barbequed, fresh cut French fries with the skin still on, and sandwiches crammed with half a chicken. Everything was greasy and salty. It was impossible to order the wrong thing from the menu. My mouth watered from thoughts of the menu and smells coming from the kitchen. I glanced around and checked the door. *They'd better be here soon, I'm starving.*

The place was dead for a Sunday night. A couple of people eating and four college guys, summer strays as we called them, must've come up to Elliot Lake for the last weekend before school. Completely wasted, they were trying to play pool, in between cat-calling the waitress. *Poor Abigail.* One of them, tall with shaggy blond hair, tried to swat her ass, but she sidestepped and strolled back to the bar rolling her eyes.

I'd settled into a booth near the far side, facing the front doors. Sort of watching the entrance, interested in the hall more than anything else. The stuffed animals on the walls kept watching my every move. Or maybe watching the door as well.

"Dude!" Seth's booming voice made everyone turn. He smiled, but then grimaced when he passed the kitchen and pinched the bridge of his nose.

Kieran strolled right behind him, dressed in dark clothes and hands in his back pockets. He surveyed the room with a bored look, shaking his head at the animals hanging on the walls.

Seth dropped into the booth. "Abi! Can we get a pitcher of Ginger ale over here?"

"Ginger ale? What are you, ninety?" I laughed. "You getting anything to eat?"

"Nah, the kitchen's got a funky odour coming out of it." He rubbed his nose, as if trying to block the smell.

"I never noticed." Kieran pulled a stool to the booth and sat down.

"Me neither. I'm starving." I grabbed the menu, already knowing what I'd order.

Abigail dropped the jug and glasses off and stood behind Kieran. "D'you guys want anything?" Her tray rested against her hip.

Loud laughter from the college boys muffled my stomach's loud grumble.

Zoe, Heidi, and Rylee slipped around Abigail and scooted into the booth. Zoe sat beside me, the other two by Seth.

Zoe grinned and whispered, "I bet Brent orders the mega-burger." She rested her elbow on the table, hands covering her ears.

I stared at her, trying to keep my eyes from wandering over her sun-kissed skin and down her short white skirt. *If I touched her skirt, would I be able to see through it?* Shaking my head, I took a deep breath and forced my fingers to play with the napkin wrapped around the cutlery. "Maybe I'm not hungry."

She gave a half-smile. "Liar. I heard your stomach growl." Her cheeks turned a shade of red that matched her low-cut tank top.

How'd she hear it? "Fine, you win." I turned to Abigail, my gaze roaming once more over Zoe's perky boobs before moving on to Abigail. *A guy's gotta look, right?* "Can I get the mega with a side of onions rings?"

Abigail blew her bangs, looking tired. "Anyone else?"

Kieran ordered the mega too, and the girls got the nacho tray.

"Seth?" Rylee said. "Anything? Or everything on the menu?"

He inhaled and turned three shades of green. "Nah, I'm good. Wait. Maybe another ginger ale? With a spoon for the bubbles." He rested his chin on his hand, his fingers covering his mouth and nose.

"If you got the flu and gonna puke..." Heidi scooted away from him and closer to Rylee.

"I'm fine... I think." Seth spoke from behind his hand. "Everything just smells totally strong. Some of it's nice, but some of it..." He gagged and shuddered as he swallowed. "I think the mine poisoned my gut."

Heidi and Rylee jumped out of the booth. Heidi slid beside Zoe, who moved closer to me. Rylee grabbed a stool and sat beside Kieran.

Seth smirked and sat up, not sick or poisoned at all. "I'm fine now." He stretched a leg out on the bench and grinned.

"Bugger," Rylee said. "You just wanted the seat to yourself. I should've seen that coming."

"*Bugger*?" Zoe asked. "Where'd that come from?"

Rylee shrugged. "Someone said it on Corrie Street or Queer as Folk or some other BBC show I watched online. It's a cool word."

Kieran laughed and crossed his arms over his chest. He winked at the girls sitting by me. "Never had someone try an' impress me that'a way. Thar's a first." His accent made his r's roll. *Great, more things to make the girls ogle over him.*

Heidi coughed, looked at Zoe, and then me. "What's going on? With all of us?"

Suddenly my skill went from being cool to dropping a stone in the pit of my stomach. *It's wrong? Wait. Do they have it too?*

Abigail's arrival with our food stopped me from replying. Taking forever, she finally set everything down and walked toward the pool tables.

I stared at my tower of onion rings, thinking about how to ask my buddies without sounding out of my mind. I grabbed the top ring and popped it into my mouth. The frown on Zoe's face stopped me from reaching for another. "What's up?"

She nodded to the college guys. "They're saying things. Pretty disgusting stuff about Abi. I hope Max kicks them out. They're gross."

"You mean Skinny, Dipshit, and Bleach-head?" Seth jabbed his thumb and smiled, looking all proud of thinking up the nicknames.

I cocked my head. All I heard was loud laughter. "How can you hear them?"

Zoe stared at her nachos. All of us grew quiet – a weird, almost knowing silence. She whispered, "I can hear everything."

"Git out," Kieran said.

"There's a guy talking outside on his cell. He's about to come in."

We all turned to the entrance and watched some guy walk in with a phone stuck to his ear. I turned to Zoe. She covered her ears, as if trying to drown out the noise.

"Your ears are wacked! My hands and feet—"

"These nachos taste like a dirty ashtray." Heidi cut me off. She pushed her plate away, her face four shades of green.

Seth leaned forward, oblivious to what had just happened. He sniffed. "They stink a bit like smoke, but better than the lard stench coming out of the kitchen." He tried a nacho, then slid the plate in front of him. "If you're not gonna eat..."

"Time out, time out, guys." I made a capital "T" with my hands. Kieran eyes jotted over each of us. *He's thinking what I'm thinking.* My head ticked like the second hand on a clock at each of my friends. *Seth complaining stuff smells bad, Zoe can hear a pin drop, Heidi's taste is off and...*

My stomach tightened, and breathing became a challenge. "All of you been weird since last night?" I scratched my jaw as each of them nodded. *All, but Kieran.* "Rylee, what's your deal? Is it your skin?"

She blinked. "No. My skin's fine but my eyes are super focused. Remember last year when I had laser surgery? It was awesome 'cause I could see everything without my glasses." She blinked, her eyes shooting everywhere around the hall. "It felt like that again this morning. Except now I can see the trees with five thousand leaves, their veins and the bugs crawling on them." She paused. "And watch the sap running through them. I swear I could see *all of it.*"

"So," I said slowly. "You've got perfect vision? And Zoe's got sensitive hearing, Heidi's taste buds are off, and Seth's nose stinks." *I thought I had sight, but it's feel. My hands and feet... it's based on my skin.* My heart pounding, I continued, my words now tumbling out, "I woke with some wicked feeling-thing in my hands. I touched a wall and *could see through it.* Same thing with the floor, like some kinda X-ray vision." I turned to the Scotsman. "What about you?"

Kieran chuckled. "Yer serious, aren't you?" He pretended to sniff, cupped an ear with his hand, and then licked ketchup off a French fry. He shook his head as he ran a finger across the table, and then rubbed his eyes and blinked a bunch of times. "Nothin'. Had a bad headache, but tha' was it. But no super-power." He leaned forward. "Yer pullin' me leg, right?"

"No joke. I can see through walls." "I can't stop hearing everything." Zoe and I spoke at the same time.

"Our senses are all screwed up," Zoe whispered. She spoke, tapping a finger with each word, "Smell, sight, taste, touch and hearing." Her eyes grew huge. "M-My dad's doing some blood work to check for radium and whatever other shit's running through me."

I put my arm around her shoulders and gave a squeeze. Her skin felt amazingly soft, but cool as if it needed my arm there. "Something weird happened after the lightning."

Heidi looked ready to cry. "It doesn't make sense. If there was radioactivity in that room last night, our skin should be falling off our bones."

"But it isn't." *What had happened in the mine?*

"Do you remember the weird smell last night?" Heidi asked.

"Yeah, can't get it out of my nostrils at the moment." Seth wiped his nose with the sleeve of his shirt.

"It was from the lightning. It's actually ozone."

Heidi's school book reading kicking in.

"Lightning splits water molecules in the air and three molecules of oxygen bond to form ozone during a lightning storm."

"Where'd the heck you learn tha'?" Kieran, the only one eating, held his burger halfway to his mouth.

Heidi shrugged. "Earth Science. Chemistry."

"Okay." Kieran didn't sound too sure.

"Heidi's got a photographic memory," Zoe explained.

"No shite?"

We all nodded. It'd been like this since second grade.

"Something happened to us while we were in that room," Heidi insisted.

This is wrong, in so many ways. "Maybe from the lightning, or the uranium mine," I said.

"I bet it was from when we were blue," Rylee added.

"Then why didn't he," Seth said, pointing at Kieran, "not get affected? Why just us?"

Kieran leaned forward and set his burger down. "Maybe you guys have some defunked gene from living in Elliot crap-hole." He held up a hand. "Sorry, mates. 'Didn't mean that like it sounded." He bit into a French fry and chewed. "Maybe something's in the water or the soil you guys absorbed. Remember, I just got here."

"You might be right," I said. "The five of us had been friends since first grade. Maybe there's something in the soil and then when the storm hit – or we got hit in the mine – it messed everything up." I shook my head, totally confused. "Can this really be happening?"

Seth straightened. "Five senses and there's five of us. And dude," he said, looking at me, "it's totally happening."

Everyone sat silent and barely moving. Except Kieran, who kept on eating his burger and fries.

Zoe let out a long sigh. "So, what do we do? Should we tell someone? Maybe my dad?"

"Heck no!" Seth pounded the table with his fist. "Think of all the crap we're gonna get away with this year at school. Getting straight A's, some serious pranks, there's so much shit. We're not screwed or dying, we just got hit with some awesome super-ability." He stared at each one of us. "So we gotta keep this our little secret."

"Little?" Heidi asked.

Seth shrugged. "Fine. Our big-ass secret. I say we don't tell anyone." He turned to Kieran. "Can you to that?"

Kieran raised his hands in mock surrender. "Don't worry 'bout me. I'm not tellin' a soul. I want ta see what you kin do with yer new bits."

"I think we should tell my dad." Zoe took a sip of her Coke. "I mean, what if something's wrong? He's already doing my blood work. I could tell him about my hearing." She chewed her lip.

Heidi spoke, "What if we get cancer or some growth or worse..."

"Like what?" Rylee said. "We wake up dead one morning?"

Everyone laughed. *Gotta deal with the nervousness somehow.*

"We tell your dad if we have to," Seth said. "If he says something about the blood results, we go from there,"

"Or we get sick," Heidi said, not sounding convinced.

"Sounds good to me," Seth said. "I don't want to be smellin' crap all the time." He sniffed. "Actually, I think it's getting better. When we were all scared, I could smell somethin' weird. Now it's changed – a bit sweeter." He scratched his head.

"Maybe you can smell fear and joy and all that shite." Kieran reached over and grabbed the pitcher. He shook the empty jug and glanced behind him. "Where's our waitress?"

I looked around. The college guys were gone, and Abigail probably went out to have a smoke break.

A sharp intake of breath beside me made the hair on the back of my neck spring up. Zoe grabbed my arm with a vice-like grip.

Don't be hurt. "What's wrong?" I asked.

Color drained from her face and her lips trembled. One shaky finger tugged at her earlobe. "Abi's in trouble."

Chapter 7

Zoe

Get away. Leave me alone! Abi's cries rang inside my ears.

Grab her. Shut her up, dammit. A male voice hissed. One of the college kids playing pool! Earlier Seth had referred to him as Dipshit.

My heart hammered against my chest. As my skin froze, I didn't think I could move if I tried. My brain had to process the thought of speaking. I wished I could turn my ears off to stop the sounds from another room in PHP.

"Ow! That's some grip." Brent shifted slightly away, and I realized I had his arm crushed between my fingers. I managed to release my grip—only to bring my hands to cover my mouth in horror.

"What's wrong, Zoe?" Brent's voice bellowed against my eardrum.

"You don't have to shout." I frowned, trying to focus on what was going on around me. The far-off voices kept pulling me back.

Brent leaned back, surprised. "I didn't. I whispered."

Pressing my palms hard against the table, I shot up. I could barely choke out the words. "A-Abi's h-hurt... but they're p-planning something worse."

"Who are?" Kieran touched my shoulder. His hand warm on my frozen skin. "Where?"

"I can hear them."

"Who?" Kieran repeated, more urgently this time.

I chewed my lip, paranoid *they* might be able to hear me. "Those college guys," I whispered.

Seth slid out of the booth, faster than I thought possible. I watched, dazed. He sniffed the air around him. "Those bastards." He punched a fist into his other hand. "I can smell their stinkin' lust. It reeks."

Rylee stood. "You can hear them, and they're not even in the room? And Seth can smell them?" She squinted and stared across the room. "They're not here. Only empty beer bottles where they were playing pool.

Brent started pushing Heidi and me out of the booth. "We've got to help her."

"Why?" Rylee said. "How about the girls stay here and call the cops. You boys go be heroes."

"Uh-uh. All of us, together." Kieran said firmly, then looked at me. "D'you got your cell? Call the cops while we're looking for them." He grabbed a pool queue and broke it in half across his knee.

I stared at him in surprise.

Me first.

No way! I'll break her in.

No way, dude. You made her ugly, so you go last.

Fuck off!

I hunched over and covered my ears, wishing I could block the college jerks talking and laughing over Abi's whimpering. Being forced to listen to something so purely evil shook me to the core.

Shut up, asshole! You're too wasted to get it up. This bitch is mine.

I cringed at the sound of a zipper, followed the sickening noise of clothes ripping.

Ow! Bitch just bit me!

Flip her over. That way she can't bite or kick.

Enough! We had to stop this. *If it were me...* I couldn't finish the thought. I grabbed the closest hand and started pulling. "We've got to find Abi. They're gonna rape her. She's somewhere inside here."

"Let's go." Kieran pulled me behind him. It was his hand I'd grabbed. He stepped back to let Brent lead the way. Heidi pulled her phone out and began dialing nine-one-one.

Terrified about what we were going to find, but horrified about what would happen if we did nothing, I followed beside Kieran still holding his hand. *They're just college guys... who will probably kick our asses.* But at least then Abi would be safe.

Brent began touching walls, pausing a mere moment at each room.

When he stumbled, Rylee hissed, "Geez, Brent. Tie your shoelace. You're not four."

Just like Rylee to think about anything but what's really going on.

Brent ignored her and with his hand, motioned me to stand beside him. I left the warmth of Kieran's hand and slipped ahead. Seth moved in behind me.

"Are their voices getting louder?" He spoke barely above a whisper, but I could hear him clearly.

I cocked my head and closed my eyes. Their voices were crystal clear, but I couldn't tell if we were any closer. "I don't know." My eyes welled so I blinked rapidly. *Useless! I can hear them, but can't find them?* I wished we were anywhere but here. "Can you see anything, Rylee? Or Seth, is their smell any stronger?"

Seth grunted. "I smell them, alright, but it ain't helping none."

Rylee shook her head. "I can't see though walls."

Brent continued walking and tripped on his untied lace again. His hands flew out to catch himself. He shot up faster than a jackrabbit. His voice shook as he spoke, "They're below us. We've got to hurry!"

Kieran ran in front of us. He did a three-sixty then pointed the broken pool cue to a barely-noticeable handle on the wall. "There."

"You sure?" Heidi shuttered to a stop.

Kieran shrugged, pressing forward and grabbing the handle. "No. Just a gut f-fe... a guess." He pulled the handle, but nothing happened.

"I don't know how I missed seeing it." Rylee spoke quietly behind me. "Push, not pull."

Kieran pushed. The door opened a crack and slammed back shut. He nodded at Seth and together they rammed their shoulders against it.

"Ow! Hey!" A guy wedged behind the open door shouted. "What the f—"

Kieran cut the guy's words off with his fist. He slumped behind the door, his legs sprawled out.

The temperature began to drop as I led the girls behind Kieran, Brent, and Seth down the dark steps toward the light in the basement. Kegs of beer, cases of wine, and massive bags of potatoes lay stacked against the walls as we stepped further in.

Skinny, Dipstick, and Bleach-head's voices screamed in my head. Soon they were loud enough the others could also hear them.

Don't let go of her leg, idiot. I plan on having a taste of this sweet thing.

Shit! Did you hear something?

Runny scaredy-pants. Try the concrete step over there by the stacked kegs. Take one of them to the car while you're at it. I'm going to show this girl what a real man feels like.

Brent and Seth leapt off the rest of the stairs.

Rounding a stack of beer kegs, we saw Abigail on the floor, her head away from us, and her skirt thrown over her back with her pale butt cheeks smudged with dirty handprints. She flailed and twisted, kicking one leg like an enraged donkey. Her other leg was trapped by Dipstick.

I couldn't see Abigail's face. Some spotty ass had his pants around his ankles. *The boy who thinks he's a damn man.* Gasps from Heidi and Rylee whirled like tornadoes in my ears.

Kieran raised the pool cue and hammered the half-naked guy across the back of his head. He fell on the ground, not moving.

Brent went after Dipstick, who still held Abi's leg. Seth knocked out the skinny guy running for the loading dock door. Brent didn't have it so lucky. His opponent grabbed a bottle of wine and slammed it against a pillar. The red wine dripped onto the concrete like blood from a severed artery. He slashed the jagged edges in the air close by Brent's face. Brent ducked and stepped back. The guy swaggered toward him, an ugly sneer on his face. He swung again and Brent bent forward, diving for the guy's legs. The bottle went flying and crashed against a keg. As they tumbled to the ground, Seth grabbed Dipstick's arms and pinned them behind his back. He thrashed around like an upside down bug.

"You smell like ass." Seth pulled the guy's arm tighter and turned his head away. He leaned toward the spilled bottle of wine, taking deep breaths.

Abigail scrambled away from the fighting bodies and broken glass. She pushed her skirt down and hid behind me and Rylee, sobbing with her head in her hands. "Thank-you, thank-you, thank-you," she mumbled repeatedly between sobs and hiccups.

Heidi had her phone out, shouting at the police. *We're getting to be regulars with the emergency departments First the mine, now this. Jeez.*

I turned around and put my arms around Abi. The tiny waitress stared up with eyes large and shocked. Her terrified, dirty, tear-streaked face burned an image into my mind. *Never again. We can't let this happen ever again.* She fell against my shoulder, sobbing uncontrollably.

Kieran stepped over the unconscious guy and gave him a kick in the gut. He walked over to the group struggling on the floor. He jabbed the broken end of the pool cue against Dipstick's neck. Bright red blood began running and staining his white shirt. The guy's heart rate exploded into a rapid rhythm.

I held my breath. We all did.

Kieran hissed, his head close enough so only Dipstick could hear... and me. "Give up, or I'll shove this up yer ass 'n pull it out the other end." The tone and venom in Kieran's voice scared the crap out of me. College dude went limp. Kieran straightened. "Funny 'ow things change when yer on the other end, eh?"

The bleach-blonde, his pants still around his ankles, moaned and pushed himself onto his knees. "What the hell? You freakin' high school pricks think..." he paused to cough blood and something white flew out of his mouth. *A tooth?* "I'm gonna kill all of you and then piss—" Without a second thought, I grabbed an almost empty bag of potatoes and swung. The distinct *thunk* against his head and back felt gratifying. He fell face-first into the dirt floor, unconscious again.

I looked at Skinny. He sat huddled in the corner, hugging his knees, his eyes bloodshot and terrified.

"The guy by the door?" Seth called out.

Rylee turned around, and stared up the darkened stairs. "He must've taken off. I was watching him—"

"You can see in the dark?" Seth asked.

"Yeah. He was there a second ago when I checked, barely moving. I turned when Zoe slammed the guy with the diddlydee potatoes."

About to ask her what the heck she meant, I saw the brand label on the bag. *Diddlydee's? Figures.* A car door slamming and engine revving distracted my train of thought. I held my breath and focused on my ears. *The guy from behind the door.* His car pulled out and my ears had no trouble catching the sound of squealing tires. "He's gone." *Sirens.* The police are coming." I shivered, either from the dampness of the basement or the horrific scene around me. I didn't know which.

"What did you say happened, um..." The policeman flipped back a page in his little notebook. "Kieran?"

Kieran shifted and shoved his hands into his jean pockets. "Those college guys were drunk when we got 'ere. The waitress seemed uncomfortable and... and when Heidi didna see her and those losers disappeared, we got paranoid an' decided ta check if everything was all right."

Brent stepped forward. "We saw the door to cellar open and heard Abi's cries." He shrugged. "We did what we had to do."

"The door was open?" The policeman's eyebrows shot up. "It's got an automatic shut-release."

Oh no. How're we going to explain this? I heard every one of my friends' heart rates speed up.

Seth laughed. "No shit?" He coughed. "Sorry. I just meant those dudes must've broke it."

The policeman crossed his arms over his massive chest. "It's just surprising you heard them and noticed *everything* going on. It's very keen for... for—"

"For a bunch of high school kids?" Kieran finished. *Nice one!*

The policeman closed his pad, having the decency to look embarrassed. "If we need any more information, we'll contact you."

After the police left, Max set us up with on-the-house hot chocolates. He thanked us profusely for protecting Abi and his bar. We sat in the same booth again, sipping from our mugs.

"Could use a beer instead," Seth muttered. He sat between Heidi and Rylee, swirling the dark liquid with a spoon.

"Me, too." Kieran sat beside me, Brent on the other side.

"I can't believe that just happened." Rylee rubbed her eyes. "My folks are never gonna let me out of the house again."

"Tonight was probably just a fluke. Nothing ever happens in this town. What are the chances?" Brent reached over and patted her hand.

"I don't agree ..." Seth spoke slowly, twirling the liquid in his mug. "I... I think we've an obligation here." His face serious. "We've got these supernatural senses now. I think we need to do something. You know, like train and focus." He grinned his typical Seth grin. "Own them."

"Until they wear off," Heidi said.

"Will they?" I asked. Part of me hoped it'd happen tonight. Another part, for some strange, crazy reason, didn't want it to ever wear off.

"Yer jokin', right?" Kieran looked around the table at all of us, his eyes finally settling on Seth. His eyebrows mashed together. I followed his gaze. "You wan' ta do this again?"

"I'm serious." Seth straightened, his knees bumping on the underside of the table. "No one knows we've got these skills. We could be... heroes."

"You read too many comic books," Brent said.

"We could train, and get outfits –"

"Costumes, you mean." Rylee laughed.

"I'm not wearing spandex." Heidi smiled for the first time this evening. "It'll be bagging on me no matter what size."

"I'm serious, guys. We—" Seth set his mouth in a tight line when Max walked over to our table.

"I'd like to thank you again." Max's eyes glistened. "Anytime you come in, the food's on me. I can't believe you got to her in time." Max wiped his hands on his apron. "Of all nights I leave the bar for half an hour. I make it back just as the cops are pulling in."

Nobody spoke. It seemed we couldn't meet each other's gazes. The silence began to get uncomfortable. I could hear all our bodies shifting and bumping into each other erratically. Somebody needed to say something.

"Th-Thanks, M-Max," I stuttered. "We... we just saw Abi go down the hall and those guys following her. It didn't seem right." I hoped the excuse worked. I didn't want special attention because of this. Abi's shattered face flashed before my mind. *Maybe Seth has a point.* I definitely didn't want that to happen to someone else.

"If you hadn't been here..." Max heaved an enormous breath out. "I don't know what would've happened. You saved the day." He shook his head as he collected our mugs and returned to the bar.

Seth leaned forward. "See. We *are* heroes. Tomorrow we need to start training. Then every day after school."

"How're we going to train? We blindfold you and make you smell things? I do taste testing?" Heidi said.

"No. We gotta learn to focus and zone in on it. It's bigger than just one sense for each of us. Wayyyy bigger."

"Where will we train that nobody in this town is gonna ask what the heck we're doing? It's not like we can hide all us." Rylee shrugged and shook her head.

"Back at the mine?" Seth asked.

"No!" I jerked at the volume of my own voice inside my head. "You couldn't drag me back in there. I'm not going inside there ever again."

"How 'bout my place?" Brent said softly. "We've got a basketball court outside and the gymnasium inside. My folks'll never care. Shoot, my dad only built the thing so he could have some charity fundraiser once a year. He's got offices in the back but nobody but me and Nate go in the gym now."

No one spoke. I heard everyone agree simply by their body language.

"It's settled then," Seth said. "Tomorrow afternoon, at two. Forget saving the day, we're gonna save the world."

Chapter 8

The radar sense of my hearing seemed to sharpen at night. It kept me waking constantly. One minute I'd bolt up, terrified by someone moaning and then gag when I realized it came from the neighbour's wife with her husband. *Ick! Disgusting!* Several deep breaths to slow my racing heart couldn't erase the image forming in my mind. Just when I managed to drift back to sleep, a car screeching, or a diesel truck flew by. Sirens, horns, animals, laughter, crying... all of it kept me from sleeping. Earplugs didn't help; nothing did.

Screw saving people. After a night of no sleep, I was more interested in killing them for some peace and quiet. By lunch time I couldn't wait to head to Brent's—anything to work off the crazy jitters and figure out a way to get my hearing to focus less. I sent Seth a text and offered to pick him up; silly to drive two cars when I went right by his place.

I pulled in Seth's driveway and killed the ignition. Slamming the Volkswagen's door, I grimaced at the rusty creaking of its hinges. As I turned to walk up the drive, a motorbike parked near the house made me pause. *Whose is that?* Seth's dad definitely didn't ride, but it wouldn't surprise me if his mom had taken up a new hobby. I grinned. She struck me as one tough woman. If I ever had kids, I hoped to be just like her.

Seth stepped out of the two-story house and onto the covered porch. "Hey!" he hollered, or so it seemed to me. Resting his hands on the railing, he leaned over.

"Your mom buy a bike?" I asked, stopping at the bottom of the stairs.

A deep laugh erupted behind him. I tried to catch a glimpse of whoever sat on the cedar chair. It was impossible to see because of the brick pillar and Seth's big, muscled body. The laugh made my stomach twist and flip. It echoed against my head making my body tingle and warm. *Weird.*

"Yer mum would ride a bike?" Kieran laughed again. He appeared at the top of the steps wearing a white tee shirt and a pair of shorts with a Scottish logo near the bottom. He stood two steps above me so the Rangers Football Club emblem hit me eye level.

"Probably," Seth scoffed, "after she sees yours. Wanna know where she is today?" He rolled his eyes at me. "Bungee jumping! What forty-five-year-old woman does that?" He tried to sound embarrassed, but the right side of his mouth turned up and he pretended to stare off at nothing to show indifference.

I knew him too well, he loved him mom and her sense of adventure. "What'd your dad say?"

"He's videotaping it!"

As Seth rambled on and walked past us toward the car, Kieran winked at me.

I smiled back. *He totally gets it.*

"My car's a bit of an antique." I pointed to the Bug, like I should apologize for her. The yellow paint and rust blended in so well together now, you couldn't tell where one ended and the other began. It looked like a tree in autumn, and I still loved it.

"Yer parents buy it fer you?" He strolled beside me, his knuckles brushed against my hand as our arms swung with walking.

"Nope." Momentarily distracted by his touch, I stuttered, "I-I bought it with money saved from a paper route I'd had since I was, like, ten. After passing my driver's license test, my dad took me to this old farm out of the city and I paid cash for her." I patted the hood, unable to hide the pride in my voice or stop myself from babbling. "I know it's kinda old."

"It's eclectic," he said.

My heart swelled. *Cute and a sense of humour.* I realized I was staring when Kieran's heart shifted its rhythm. "So... anything going on with you? You know... with the sensation-thing?"

He shook his head. "Nothing, but it's okay. I'm here ta watch, and cheer you on. I'm yer biggest fan." He rubbed his shoulder against mine. "I'll be your guys' groupie."

"You comin' or what?" Seth stood behind the open passenger door, one leg already inside the car. "I call shotgun."

Kieran crawled into the back behind the driver's seat. I hopped in and started the engine. I shoved the stick shift into reverse and popped the clutch. Our eyes met in the rearview mirror as I backed out the driveway. He was smoking-hot. I loved his slightly messy dark hair that my fingers begged to let me run themselves through it. Thin and soft, but any girl knew there had to be power behind them.

I made a mental effort to focus back on the road, wondering if Kieran or Seth could hear my thoughts. They seemed to shout so blatantly inside my mind. Crap, I probably had a neon sign above my head: "I'm hot for the Scot."

"Brent's place is perfect," Seth said, interrupting my thoughts. He threw his arm over my seat and turned back to look at Kieran. "His folks are loaded. His granddad left a crap-load of money to his dad. Actually, I think he left a crazy amount to Brent and his brother, Nate, as well. Anyway, his dad's some kind of genius and invested the money to make a shit-load more. I think they use hundred dollar bills to line their coffee filter every morning."

Kieran laughed. "I'll check the toilet paper roll while I'm there, as well."

Appalled to hear Seth talk like that about Brent, I threw him a dirty look and thrust my hand out and thumped him across the chest. "He's your best bud, and you dis him?"

"Hey!" Seth blocked his upper body with his arms, expecting me to hit him again. "I was braggin'. Brent's totally cool. He doesn't act like big money." He turned again to Kieran. "I can't say it doesn't suck being his buddy, though. Dude's always footin' the bill, always got my back. The only other thing he spends money on is his guitar collection."

I glanced at the rearview after turning into Brent's long driveway. "He's an awesome guitar player. He's played at PHP a couple times."

"Cool." Kieran turned his head to the window and whistled. "Nice pad."

The huge red brick house sat on too many acres to count. It was one of those monstrous old estates Brent's dad had moved from somewhere near Niagara Falls and brought here. The entire thing had been redone, with an awesome white porch you wished you had, except it would never fit on your own house.

Whenever I stepped inside, I couldn't believe the massive size of each room, with twenty-foot ceilings, walnut floors, and working fireplaces in, like, every room. Brent's mom liked antique stuff so she'd filled the house with old and new. It looked pretty cool, but I doubt Brent and his brother ever got to run or play inside.

"His mom's a fashion designer," I told Kieran. "She wants Brent to have our grad party here. He only agreed, if it's in the gym. *He's*," I shot Seth a warning glare, "not into showing off, but would do anything for his mom." Brent was a really sweet guy, and always had my back. So I returned the favour.

"Wait till you see this billion dollar gym. It's freakin' aw—"

I nailed Seth again in the chest, harder this time.

"Okay!" He held his hands up in surrender. "Just make this Bug crawl a bit faster and pull around back."

I drove to the end of the drive and parked the car in the lot at the side of the gym. *This place is totally brag-worthy.* Massive, with an NBA-sized basketball court, a weight room that made any gym seem cheap, ten-person sauna, and probably more I'd never noticed. It put the only school in town's gymnasium to shame.

Brent stood outside with his back against the brick. When I stopped, he strolled over and put his hand on the Bug. His fingers were spread wide, his brows scrunched together in concentration. He'd touch the car, pull his hand away, and then touch it again – from one end of my little car to the other.

"Sheesh, Zoe." He chuckled. "You got trash in your front trunk, crap under the driver's seat, and I think there's a mouldy sandwich."

Seth laughed. "What, feel-boy? You can't see it clear enough? I can sure smell it."

Brent kept a straight face. "Things so mouldy I can't tell if it's food or if it's your mother's underwear from last time I took her out for a drive."

Kieran and I died laughing. "That... is disgusting!" I choked out.

Seth swung his door open and set his long legs on the pavement. He stood and stretched, inhaling deeply. "Smells like money," he mumbled. I heard him clear as day. He pointed to Brent. "I'm gonna let that one slide only 'cause I know I'll kick your ass when we get inside." He grinned and crossed his arms over his chest.

I jumped out and swung my worn seat against the wheel, grabbing it just before it hit the horn. For a little old car, my horn blasted like a semi-truck's. *Not so good for the elephant-ear girl.*

Kieran brushed against me as he squeezed by. "Ta."

I fought to control myself. *One word and I'm mush?*

"T-The girls here yet?" I asked Brent, trying to distract myself.

He tipped his head back. "Yeah, they're playing around in the gym. Rylee's built some wicked obstacle course. She got all excited when she found the storage room with the gymnastic equipment."

"Awesome!" Seth slammed his door. "What have they all done?"

"They kicked me out." Brent shrugged. "Said they wanted to surprise us."

"Did you peek?" I lightly tapped his wrist with my finger.

Brent pretended to stare up at the sky. I tapped harder.

"Maybe a couple of times." He laughed.

"Come on, aren't you loving the skills?"

"Yeah!" Seth bellowed. "This is going to be amazing!"

"I don't get how doing exercise is going to change things?" Kieran asked.

"It's not the working out." Seth flexed. "But it does help with attracting the ladies." He relaxed his stance when he caught my glare. "Watch us on the stuff and see what happens. Let's go! No time like the present to change the world." He ran over to the door, disappearing behind it.

We followed, but at a slightly less neck-breaking speed.

"Any changes, Kieran?" Brent asked.

"I wish." Kieran sighed. "It's daft, but I got nothing."

I loved the bounce of Kieran's words as he spoke. Imagine having his voice on the radio. I'd listen to it all night long. Shame I had to listen to annoying humming sounds from inside the building and every bird and animal within a five mile radius along with Kieran's accent. Nearly walking into the door, I caught myself just in time. *Nobody notice, please.* Inside, I blinked, my eyes adjusting to the gym. My ears picked up strange building noises immediately. The purr of the fans, the whirring of the electrical power to the lights, an air conditioner... everything I'd heard outside, only louder now.

Rylee came running over to hug each of us. "I got a little carried away." She pointed behind her. "If Brent's dad doesn't care, we could keep this up for a while and practice our skills here."

Brent shrugged. "Not a problem."

"How long've you been here?" I asked. She'd hung climbing ropes, built an obstacle course, gymnast spring mats at one side, a punching bag, and some other hitting bag beside it. Rylee pushed a red button on a remote in her hand and the Rocky soundtrack started blaring out of the speakers. I jerked in surprise.

"Too loud?" she mouthed and hit the volume button down a tiny bit. "Better?"

"Sorta." I walked toward the wall console and manually turned it down a few more notches. Rylee went over to Seth and began talking excitedly, pointing at all the equipment. In one corner, Rylee had erected a twenty-foot pole diagonally into the air with stacked blocks and a ladder. *Not lookin' too stable.* I stared, wondering what the heck she planned on having us do with it. Heidi sat stretching on the blue mats.

Seth clapped his hands loudly together. "It's time to turn ourselves into superheroes."

We all laughed, Kieran loudest of all. "What's yer plan?"

Seth's face remained serious. "We've got these super senses. They're going to make our physical attributes stronger, as well."

Heidi patted him on the back, and teased, "Wow! Three syllables. I think that's the biggest word you've ever used."

Seth beamed as he elbowed Heidi. She had to jump out of the way or fall over. "See, it's working already. I'm getting smarter as we speak."

Brent and I looked at each other and rolled our eyes.

"I saw that," Seth said, but I could hear there was no anger in his voice.

"How d'you figure? That yer senses are going ta make you stronger?" Kieran leaned against a wall, his arms tucked snugly against his chest.

"Let me show you." Seth stepped forward and grabbed one of the long, thick ropes hanging from the ceiling.

Heidi wrinkled her nose and coughed. "Not to be the kid with the photographic memory," she said, "but these super senses might interfere with physical prowess because of the endocrine system's reaction to the heightened stimuli. Like a disproportionate overload, and," her eyes flitted over each of us, "Oh, never mind."

We all stared, open-mouthed.

"I'm just guessing." She grinned, probably because she'd grown used to our confused faces. "So, where do we start?"

"Everywhere... Anywhere," Seth replied. "Pick a station and start." He pointed to his right. "Try the rock climbing wall and see how easy it'll be for you now. Or have a go at the punching bag... whatever." One hand still on the rope, he reached above it with his other hand and began climbing. In a flash he reached the top, grinned down at us, and swung his body to move the rope back and forth. In reach of the adjacent rope, he grabbed it with a free hand. *What the –? How'd he do that so fast?* He slid down the two, one hand on each side, his feet set so the ropes slid around his ankles. When he dropped to the ground, he laughed. "See? Easy as pie."

"I don't believe you." I walked over and grabbed his wrists. "You've got to have blisters and rope burn from sliding like that." Flipping his hands over so the palms were up, I stared in amazement. *Nothing.* No burn, or redness, nothing.

He held a rope out to me. "Try it."

"I can't climb up there. I can't even do a chin-up." I grabbed his hand and looked at it again. "Your hands are probably used to this so it didn't hurt them."

"They'll start hurting, but it takes longer than normal. I've been doing some stuff at the park since the night at the mine. The crazy-strong smell thing stinks, but the stuff that comes with it... you gotta try it to believe it." Seth started up the rope again. He had tanks for biceps, but it looked like an invisible line pulled him up.

Super-strong boy can kiss my butt. Still curious, I walked over to the boxing bag. I rubbed the back of my neck, not sure how to hit the thing. *This is stupid.* Seth probably planned some stupid joke.

Ticked, my fingers curled and sucked my breath in. I could hear the others trying their stations. Rylee talking under her breath and wondering if Kieran had his eyes on her. Heidi talking quietly to

Brent about this idea being a shot in the dark.

Seth's face. My fist shot out and hit the bag, pretending to punch him. It squeaked back and forth in protest. I punched it again and tried doing that thing Rocky does in his movies. *Hit, hit, hititty hit.* Shocked, I managed to hit it dead center every time. *Take that, Mr. Balboa.*

As it swung on its little lever, a sound resonated against my ears. My head tilted to the side and I squinted.

A noise so unique it changed the way I heard things – the way I processed sound – forever.

My fist continued striking the bag as fast as it could, but the bag itself moved in slow motion. Or so it seemed. Exhaling the breath I didn't know I'd been holding, I tried alternating both hands and let it rip. I never missed. *Totally awesome.*

My knuckles felt as if they were starting to split but I wanted to keep going. When my arms began to weigh a hundred pounds each but the muscles had turn to Jell-O, I knew I needed a break. *Jell-O now, tomorrow they're going to be lead.* I let them drop to my sides.

"Guys, are you getting the same reaction I'm getting?" Brent called out. "It's weird and totally amazing."

"I-I think so," I said and moved to a station where Rylee had made some laser-thing with ropes. Each rope had a million little bells that probably sounded like sweet music to everyone's ears but more like the bells of Notre Dame Cathedral while standing under the bell to me.

Heidi came over. "You need to figure out how to get through without touching the ropes and setting the chimes off." She lightly tapped the rope closest to her, barely making it move.

Dull sounds of the metal resounded off the gentle shake of the ropes as they hung. *Just figure a way to manoeuvre a way through. That's all.* I bent and lifted a leg to squeeze through the first two ropes closest to me. Over, under and keep my balance. *No matter if I stand on one foot, a tippy-toe, or whatever—focus on your center.*

Over, under, balance. Over... under... balance. "This one's kinda fun," I said and turned to Heidi to see if she wanted to try. I blinked in surprise. "How'd I get so far?"

Heidi grinned. "I was just about to ask you the same thing."

Easy as pie. Strange for someone whose only physical activity consisted of gym class and walking. I slipped through the last section, amazed the simple tension of the ropes made the little bells move in such a way it gave me a different line of vision. "Give it a try."

Heidi took a deep breath and swallowed. She made it through the first two, and ever so slightly rubbed her shoulder against the next rope. Barely a touch, but the bells went off like a crazy house.

Covering my ears, I swung around. Waiting for the noise to turn manageable, I watched Rylee at the punching bag, Brent climbing some boxes, and Seth scratching his head. Each of them were grasping the same things I'd just realized. Everyone, but Kieran. He stood observing us, his mouth hung open.

"Hey! Watch this," Brent shouted. He'd climbed up the boxes and then the wonky ladder by the pole Rylee had set up. After touching the pole with both hands a couple of times, he then stepped on the metal and suddenly slid all the way down – like he was surfing. He jumped off at the end and fist pumped. "Freakin' amazing! Holy crap!"

If he can do it... While everyone hooted and ran over to ask him questions, I tightened my ponytail and crawled onto the boxes. On the rickety ladder my palms grew damp and I could feel sweat start along my hairline. Noise from all around bounced inside my head. *Maybe this is a little too crazy.* I paused near the final rung, unsure. The pole seemed pretty narrow, and it looked so shiny – almost slippery.

"Go for it," Kieran murmured quietly.

I glanced down at him. He smiled and mouthed, "You can do it." He must have realized I'd hear it.

Determined, I set my right foot onto the slim pole, leaning against the wall, unable to move. I wiped my hands against the side of my pants. I couldn't hear anything coming from the pole. No noise like I had heard from all the other equipment I'd tried. Lips pressed tight, I tried to think of something that might help. I stared down at my hands, my thumb playing with my high school ring on my right hand's ring finger. An idea popped into my head.

Bending down I clapped the pole with my hands, letting my ring clang against the metal. *Metal on metal.* The pole vibrated and a shudder ran down its length. No one even noticed. *No one, but me.*

The vibration created a rhythm, and as I stared in disbelief, I could see the slight movement created a larger surface as it shook. *Bigger equals better balance. Perfect – I hope.* I hit it again, and jumped on before I lost my courage.

The rush was over before I wanted it to end, like being on a longboard going down a steep stairwell banister – *No, wayyy better.* Realistically, the narrow pole was more like taut tightrope, but as I slid, it seemed more like the width of a sidewalk. It had been... easy. *Too easy.*

Comprehending what I'd accomplished, I stomped my feet and screamed, "Ewww!!"

The gang raced over laughing and cheering.

Not caring what anyone thought, I started dancing and singing. "I skated the po-ole. I'm on the edge of super, hanging on a skinny pole. I'm on the edge of hero. I'm on the edge—"

"Oh no," Rylee joked, covering her ears. "The happy dance is fine, but can you do it without the tone deaf Lady Gaga remix?"

Brent laughed and hopped beside me, bumping my hip as he joined in on the dance. "You'd think with her awesome hearing, she'd be able to carry a tune." He winked at me. "Wanna do it again – at the same time? Race the pole?" He motioned to Kieran when I nodded. "Let's make another pole. Zoe and I want to race."

Kieran clapped his hands and walked over. "Pole skating, eh? You guys made it look effortless." His gaze lingered a millisecond on me, making my heart flip-flop. "Let's make it more challenging."

"Whatever you say, coach." Rylee threw her hair back and laughed. "What do you have in mind?"

"Coach?" Kieran grinned. "I like it." He leaned forward. "How 'bout we try the water tower?"

THE END

~ to be continued ~

What's going to happen at the water tower?

Find out in:

Radium Halos Part 2

(Excerpt Chapter from Part 2 included in this book!)

Available February 28, 2014

Radium Halos Part 2

Excerpt

Radium Halos 2

~

Chapter 1

Zoe

"The water tower?" Brent scratched at the shadow of stubble on his chin. "How we going to race—?"

"Without killing yourselves?" Heidi shook her head and crossed her arms over her chest. "Uh-uh. Dumb idea."

"Wait a minute. It's a great idea." Seth began pacing with excitement. "The tower's easy triple the height of this thing in here. The city's repainting it right now so it's got all that scaffolding up."

Kieran pointed north in the direction of the old water tower. It stood more as tourist billboard off the highway than as an actual storage tank. It still carried rain water but who knew if farmers or anyone actually used it. "I drove by yesterday and noticed some slanted trough bits set up." He shrugged. "Maybe they plan to drain it or something. Thought it be perfect to race down."

Heidi sighed. "I don't–"

"I'm game." I cut Heidi off before her reasoning would convince me to change my mind. I wanted—no needed—something more challenging. *To beat Brent or impress Kieran?*

Seth grabbed his sweatshirt and shoved it on over his head. "Let's go. We can discuss it on the way."

Dusk turned dark by the time we got there and walked around the tower. At least the air was warm. The engines from the cars zooming by on the nearby highway buzzed by my ears like mosquitoes. Even with the sound barrier bricks, the noise penetrated through.

Seth tossed a pebble into the nearby trees. "It might be hard to see but it means we won't get caught. The lights from the highway are giving decent a glow but the scaffoldings on the other side."

"It's too dark and too stupid to even consider this." Heidi trailed a few feet behind us.

Rylee stopped walking and put her hands on her hips. "You stay on the ground then. Grow some kahuna's and stop bein' such a freakin' wimp."

My mouth fell open. "Rylee!" We were all nervous, but Rylee didn't need to be a bitch.

Kieran moved to Heidi and slipped his arm around her shoulders. "Don't worry, lass. You stay by me. They'll be fine. Watch and see." He pointed at all of us. "You all have the skills. Just believe. It's easy for me to see watching you, but they're there. I know it."

Silent, we walked to the other side of the tower. The tall grass had become dry and crackled under our feet. Paranoid I kept staring at the ground, positive some slinking animal would come scurrying out. I knew I'd hear it before but it still gave me the heebie-jeebies. I think we were all paranoid someone would drive by or a cop would show up. No way was getting caught part of the plan.

The scaffolding went about half way up the ball and like Kieran had said earlier, there were two long tube-like structures emptying into large disposal bins.

Brent jogged over to one of the bins and spread his fingers on the side metal. "Garbage, paint chips, cans, and other junk. They probably use the tubes instead of taking stuff down the ladders."

Seth stood under one of the troughs, jumped up and hung on. Using his large frame, he shook his weight to see if it would hold. "It's strong enough." He let go and dropped back down to the ground.

I chewed my lower lip and tried to calculate how high up the scaffolding stood. Six stories? Maybe seven? Eight? It looked pretty high. "Is it just Brent and I racing?"

Rylee climbed a few rungs of the scaffolding and hugged it tight when it lurched slightly from the wind. "How about you guys go first?" She quickly crawled back down. "Then maybe Seth and me."

I inhaled a deep breath. Cars racing down the highway roared in my ears, the wind swirling through the trees and slapping against the tower distracted me, but I wanted to do this. Adrenaline rushed through my veins and wouldn't leave till I pushed it. I reached for the cold metal and started climbing.

A minute later I glanced down to see my friends. I couldn't tell if their eyes or opened mouths were bigger. "Brent! You coming... or you chicken?" I grinned. I had one up on him, on all of them if no one else did it. I heard Heidi whisper to Rylee.

"You do know I can totally hear you. And I am not going psycho," I interrupted her. "For the record, I'm completely clear in the head." I reached inside my back pocket and tossed them my phone. "Don't drop it." I started climbing again intentionally not looking down.

I heard Brent mumble "Ah shit," under his breath and the ladder shifted and shook slightly from his weight. His increased heart rate and breathing echoed inside my ears. It didn't take him long to catch up to me.

Five minutes later we reached the flat boards of the scaffolding. I crawled through the small gap and sat down; to catch my breath...

and my courage. Brent slid beside me a moment later. I hugged my knees. He hung his legs over the edge and leaned into the lower railing. There were two railings and the boards under us were sturdy. It felt safe up here on the scaffold. The minute we stepped off would be another story.

He grinned. "You're fearless now, aren't you?"

I swallowed and rested my elbows on the railing. "Not at the moment."

"We don't have to do this."

"Trying to make me look like the wimp?" I teased. "No way. I will race you in the dark, or at a park, down the pole, or in a hole. I will not lose this race, I will not lose, Brent-I-am."

He shook his head and chuckled. "Sad. Very, very sad."

I giggled but turned quiet as I stared at the night lights of Elliot Lake and listened to the massive sounds of the night. Cars driving, people partying, watching TV, someone crying, a distinctive I love you shouted and then followed by laughter. I sighed. It felt like I was eavesdropping on everyone.

He followed my gaze. "There's something about being this high up...it's...it's..."

"I know what you mean." Words couldn't describe the incredible feeling.

The town shone with lights of the night in different colours and hues. Northern Lights seemed to be dancing along the edge of the sky. "I bet Rylee could see everything from up here."

"It amazing from what I can see." Brent cleared his throat as he looked away from me and across the county. "If her eyes are that much better, yeah, wow. As much as I want to leave here when I graduate, tonight makes me think this place ain't so bad."

I scanned the view and concentrated on the forest area not far from the water tower. "I plan on coming back when I'm done with university. It's a great place. I could grow old here."

"Like get married and have a fam—"

"Brent!" I grabbed his forearm and clenched it tight and pointed at the trees with my free hand. "Look! There towards the left."

A weird dancing light flickered a moment, then disappeared. It happened again twenty seconds later.

"What is that?" Brent began tapping his fingers against the metal railing, the noise echoed inside my ear canal. "There it is again. It's bigger. Wait. Now it's not disappearing."

A strange cracking mixed with a hissing kind of noise strained against my ear drums. I closed my eyes to focus and try to locate what the noise meant. My eyes popped open at the same moment Brent whispered, "Fire."

I reached for my phone. "Crap! My phones down at ground level."

"Mine too."

"They can't see it down there because of those huge garbage bins." I tried inhaling a few deep breaths. It suddenly felt like my brain wanted to go dizzy.

Brent reacted the second before I came back to life. He pointed to the metal tube jutting out of the corner off to my right. "You go down that one. I'll use the one by the ladder." He rested his hand on my shoulder. "We'll slide down on our stomachs, okay? Just hold tight like you're going down a stair banister." His fingers trailed down my arm. "Whatever you do, don't let go."

"I won't." I tried pushing the sudden erratic butterflies back down. "You don't go and break anything." My legs and arms moved with their own will towards my corner. "Brent?"

"Yeah?" He was crawling on his hands and knees but paused to look back at me.

"Let's not tell our dads we did this."

"Gotchya." He chuckled. "Your dad'll kill me before mine's even finished yelling." He began moving again.

I listened to Kieran, Seth, Heidi and Rylee talking below. They were arguing who should video it on their phones. They had no idea about the flames. I glanced again at the batch of trees. The flames were definitely getting bigger.

The wood boards shifted and shook slightly as all of Brent disappeared except for his hands.

I slipped my right leg through the lower railing and then my left. My hands clung tight to the railing above and I shuffled the last few inches to the trough. I squinted at it shape and crouched down. The trough was very smooth, probably about the width of my shoe.

"Screw going on my stomach," I mumbled. I clung to the rail on the scaffold with one hand and set both feet onto the hollow metal tube. I leaned like a sprinter in the starting blocks. The pole shook from the wind and gave me the feeling of a wider base. The noise created little ricochets that my ears translated into something for my eyes. Eerie silvery light. Freaky but it let the butterflies stop trying to rip through my gut to break free.

"Brent," I whispered. "Can you see?"

"A bit. Use your hearing, Zoe." Brent swallowed. "Focus on yourself. Be careful." From the corner of my eye I saw him start to slide.

I pushed against the scaffold as hard as I could. Feet set as if I was on a skateboard, I leaned forward as far as I could. It was impossible to see Brent now from my peripheral vision but he definitely wasn't in front of me anymore.

He couldn't be far behind. Our troughs were about twenty metres apart so I knew he was close, and he hadn't fallen. Keeping my abs tight, I remembered some coach or gym teacher saying our core centre of balance lay an inch or two below our belly button. Keeping it tight seemed important to maintaining balance.

The wind whipped my hair behind me and roared against my ears, along with screams from below. My eyes watered but blinking a bunch of times helped. I focussed on staring at the trough ten meters ahead. I shifted slightly when I realized the silvery misty thing I saw against the beam had a rectangular shape in front of me.

I lost balance when I realized it was the huge Waste Management garbage bin. My arms automatically spread wide and I regained equilibrium. That's when I saw Brent about two feet behind me and the gang jumping up and down with Seth and Rylee's pointed at us and cheering.

"Jump!" Kieran shouted. To me, or Brent, or maybe both of us.

I did, about half a second before I'd have landed into the bin. In the air I tucked into a ball, ready to roll when I hit the grass.

My feet hit first and all ability to gracefully roll turned into me jarring and flopping around until I finally stopped with a mouthful of grass and dirt.

"Zoe won!" Rylee cheered.

I moaned and covered my face. "Freakin' 'eh!" No blood rushed from my nose and nothing appeared broken. However, my body had landed like a train wreck.

Brent. I popped my head up. He lay on his back just behind me. He leaned up on his elbows "Holy sh—"

"Th-The f-fire!" I huffed as I tried to catch the knocked out wind. I struggled to sit up.

Seth must not have heard me. He rushed over and knelt over Brent waving his phone. "I got it all on video. I can't believe Zoe stood up and you went down it like a pansie. "

I grimaced as I touched my elbow. A bad strawberry burn with blood oozing down my arm brought me back to reality. "We raced down 'cause we saw a fire." Using my fingers, I signalled Rylee to toss me my phone. "We gotta call nine-one-one again."

"You're jokin'!" Heidi opened her mouth and breathed in. She coughed like she'd just tasted a mouthful of smoke. Doubling over, she waved in the direction behind the bins. "Call the fire department. I mean your Dad!"

Seth sniffed and started running. He disappeared behind the large metal box. I heard him tapping the numbers on his phone. "Dad! There's a fire not far from the water tower. No, it wasn't us.

We were just hanging out and saw it."

Ignoring the pain radiating from my elbow, I pushed myself up and started chasing Seth.

"What's he saying?" Heidi ran beside me.

"His dad wants to know if we saw how it started." I continued listening to Seth who was still at least four hundred meters away. "Now he wants to know why we were climbing the tower. He's giving Seth crap about the dangers and stuff."

"How bad's the fire?" Kieran shouted. He had already passed us and ran by Seth.

"I barely see it through the trees." Rylee sprinted to catch up to the boys. "But there's smoke in the air. A lot. It's moving pretty fast."

"I hear it. It's louder now than from the scaffold." Sirens started far off into the distance. Too far for my liking. I glanced behind and almost stumbled. "Where's Brent?"

A sudden gust of wind blew in our direction, full of smoke and the smell of burning. The heat of the fire heading our way suddenly made everything too real. The fire was getting incredibly close.

"What?" Seth shouted as he stopped running. He bent over with his hands on his knees. Everything inside of him was pumping and pushing and begging for more oxygen.

"Brent's not with us." Panic pressed against my chest. Had he hurt himself before and not owned up to it? I went over what happened when we'd landed only moments ago.

"He's..." Kieran glanced at Rylee who was frantically looking around. His head turned in the same direction as hers when she brought her hand to her mouth and her breath caught.

"What the heck?" She pointed to the water tower. "He's up there."

"Huh?" Seth straightened, plugged his nose and tried not to cough. "What's he doing?"

I swung around and squinted. It was hard to see but the scraping of metal and sudden banging of hollow metal couldn't be missed. One of the troughs shifted and wobbled back and forth. Just as I realized what Brent was doing, Kieran started tearing back to the water tower.

"He's gonna get the water to flood the ground and forest. We 'ave to help him!"

Those of us still standing burst into a sprint. We raced back to tower, the distance now seeming longer this time. Sirens grew louder and a fire truck flew by on the highway, its lights flashing. Another one followed him down the exit moments later.

Brent had managed to break the top of a tube I had slid down on loose from the scaffold and was rolling it.

Seth coughed and spate. "What's he doing, Rylee?"

Rylee pressed a hand against her eyebrows and looked up at. "He's got the top of the tube by a latch on the water tower. I think he's trying to hammer the handle."

To get the latch open so water would pour down. "Brent's got an idea."

"Let's get the base moved." Kieran jumped onto the bin and began kicking the base of the tube.

It took the five of us on the ground to break the trough free of the bin. It groaned in protest as it shifted a few meters. We worked without thinking or talking, all of going as fast as we could.

The noise from the fire terrified me, like it wanted to hunt us down. Heat burned against my skin and made all of us sweat. Everything was moving too fast. Ironically the ash drifted by in a slow dance.

"Pussshhh!" Seth hollered as his muscles strained in exertion. Finally the trough broke free from a tripod stand that kept it stable near the base. The bars clamoured to the ground and the trough swung away from us toward the fire.

From above Brent hollered, "Watch out!"

I heard the water bubble inside the tower and splash against the insides of the trough as it raced down. Brent must have managed to get the hatch open and set the trough to let the water pour down. I jumped up to try and push the base of the tube toward the forest. I could barely reach it now only my fingers managed to make contact. It didn't budge. "Seth! Push it again. The water's coming!"

Seth ran and leapt in the air, both arms coming up and nailing the trough with perfect athletic timing. It swung wild and water ricocheted out of the spout flying over the first trees and dumping into the forest. The trough swung a few meters to the right and, because of the pressure from the water, moving back to the left like a clock pendulum.

Angry hissing and sound of fire drowning sounded like music to my ears. "It's hitting the fire."

The same time I spoke Rylee said, "I can see it."

"Fire department's on the other side fighting it as well." Brent stood beside Kieran, his arms crossed and a big goofy grin on his face.

I ran over and hugged him. "You crazy idiot!"

"Idiot?" Kieran laughed. "I'd say more along the lines of a genius. That was brilliant." He high-fived Brent.

"I saw the lower flood latch when Zoe and I were up there before. I figured it was worth a shot. How you guys moved the base was awesome." Brent opened and closed his hands into fists, then tucked them into his jean pockets.

"See!" Seth pounded Brent on the back. "I told you we make an awesome team."

Kieran glanced toward the road. "Oye! May I suggest we get our arses outta here? Don't think we want ta get caught."

"Oh, crap!" Heidi turned and started running down the path.

Everyone followed her, only to stop and turn in the opposite direction when sirens warned us someone was coming.

We sprinted about fifty metre when gravel crunching gave me the heads up before the others. About to warn them, I never got the chance. Heidi pulled up short when a red SUV blocked the road. Rylee covered her eyes from the bright head lights.

A fireman jumped out of the driver's side and held his hand up. He held a phone in the other. "Nobody move. I'm calling the cops."

Chapter 2

Radium Halos Part 2 Excerpt

"We didn't do it." Brent walked over to Heidi.

Another fire department vehicle drove up. It lurched to a stop and Seth's dad jumped out. "You kids alright?" Another fire fighter jumped out of the passenger side and began climbing up the scaffold ladder.

"We're fine, Dad." Seth pointed to the fireman with the phone still by his ear. "He thinks we started the fire."

Rylee glanced at the dying fire and water still gushing from the tower. "We didn't."

"Russ, put the phone away. That's my kid. They're the ones who soaked the flames on this end."

Russ hit a button on his phone.

Seth didn't let Russ reply. "You saw what we did? Totally awesome, 'eh?"

His dad smiled. "Quick thinking but dangerous." He shook his head. "What were you doing out here anyway?"

Russ snorted. "Not hard to guess."

Seth's dad shot him a warning look. "Some inexperienced camper called nine-one-one and said he'd dropped a gasoline canister when trying to get a bonfire going."

Russ shook his head. "Tell your kid and his friends to get a job or find something useful to do in the evenings. Not hang out where trouble seems to be finding them." He got in his truck, slammed the door shut and spurned gravel as he drove off.

Seth's dad sighed and shook his head.

"Why couldn't you stop the fire where it started?" Seth asked his dad, refusing to acknowledge Russ' last remark.

"We got to the flames but when the wind changed direction suddenly we thought we were screwed. You kids...well, you basically saved the day."

"Saved the night." Heidi murmured.

"Superheros." Seth nudged her.

His dad either hadn't heard or purposely ignored them. "Good job but incredibly stupid and dangerous." He tapped Seth on his chest. "You better not have been drinking out here." He looked around at all of us. "You're good kids, but what in the world? The cops are going to want to know who did the damage to city property. First the mine, then PHP and now here. You guys are going to start getting the wrong reputation." He glanced up the gravel road. "I think you need to get going."

Sirens screamed further off in the distance, a different sound to the ones from the fire trucks. I glanced at the others, unsure if we should run.

Brent, on my right, stood staring at my elbow. "You need a bandage on that."

"It's fine." I tried to pull my sleeve down to hide it.

Seth's dad stopped jabbering when the fireman climbed down from the water tower and stood by the truck. The two-way inside the cab crackled to life. Police were heading to this area.

Seth's dad raced to the truck and got in. He started the engine and did the fastest U-turn I'd ever seen. As he drove by us, he rolled the window down. "Get out of here. I'll talk to the cops and make sure Russ is on the same page." He sped away after the SUV.

We did as he told and raced out there. None of spoke the ride home and back at Brent's place we gathered our things and said good night. I think everyone needed to go over the evening on their own. I know I did. So many thoughts were racing around in my head, competing with the noises in my ears and I had no idea how to calm them down.

The next afternoon I leaned against the biology room window when a bike engine roared to life. Rylee was skipping last class to leave with Kieran on his motorcycle. I heaved a disappointed sighed and couldn't stop myself watching as they zoomed off school property.

Trying to refocus my attention on memorizing the periodic table seemed next to impossible. My thoughts kept drifting back to Rylee. Her coy laughter as she climbed on the bike behind Kieran, the rustling of her hair as she tossed it over her shoulder before putting a helmet on and whispering she hoped he didn't mind her holding him super tight so she wouldn't fall.

Honestly, how could a hundred and eighteen chemical elements and their freakin' atomic structure be more important than a hot guy? I groaned. What about chemistry between people? More like the lack of it. I obviously didn't stand a chance if Kieran was even remotely interested in Rylee. Of course she'd be interested in the new guy. Who could blame her?

Kieran would have to be blind not to notice her. Straightening my arms to try and focus on the chart again, I swore under my breath when my bruised elbow rubbed against the desktop.

No way could I focus. Frustrated, I began picking up on everyone's conversations – those studying and others gossiping. *This freakin' sucks!* The guy I like is with the prettiest girl in town, I can't sleep because everything is too bloody loud, and when I get annoyed it's impossible to block anything out! I couldn't do it when I was calm and it magnified a hundred times when I wasn't. Rubbing my eyes against the palms of my hands, Heidi's tentative step echoed in my ears several seconds before she spoke. It gave me a moment to try and compose myself.

"Everything okay?" Heidi never missed anything. She even made the effort to whisper below normal levels.

None of us had mentioned last night at the water tower. Somehow all of us had made the consensus to wait till we were on our own after school. I slid the chart back and forth across the counter then stopped as the laminate screeched against the fake wood desk. I tried to make my face blank, praying it would be unreadable. "Yeah, I'm alright. It's just hard to concentrate with..." I pointed at my ears. Stretching my legs, I grimaced. "I think every muscle in my entire body has been ripped and shredded."

"After what you and Brent did last night plus training, I'm not surprised. How's your elbow?"

"Bruised and ugly." I glanced down. An icky, patchy scab surrounded by purple, green and blue skin throbbed on my skin and deeper to the muscle. It actually seemed to have scabbed over pretty quickly. "It'll heal. How are you feeling?"

Heidi swallowed and frowned. "I swear I can taste the lactic acid in my system from what we did yesterday. Are we going to Brent's again today?"

"I think so." Hopefully playing dumb worked. I did not want to appear obvious that I had just heard the motorcycle zoom away.

"I'll go, but no training crap. My arms are killing me. I can barely hold my pen." She pretended to lift her pencil like a weight bar and faked falling over. We started giggling, and then had to grab our sides at the same time from the sore muscles, which only made us laugh more. Class dragged, but at least we had each other to keep company.

After class Heidi and I met up with Seth and Brent in the parking lot by my car.

"Where's Rylee?" Seth glanced around and checked his watch.

I shifted, reminded again of the motorcycle ride.

Brent saved me from answering. "She and Kieran are changing the gym around." He opened the passenger door to the Bug. "I went by my place at lunch and turned the alarm system off. Rylee bugged me all morning. When she gets an idea in her head..." He shook his head. "She was driving me nuts." He dropped the passenger seat forward to let Heidi climb in, then straightened the seat and dropped onto it. "Let's go see if they need help."

Heidi shook her head. "She can be very persistent."

Seth crawled into the backseat from my side and groaned. "Man, Zoe. This back's so tiny for a big guy like me. I'm freakin' sore from yesterday."

Heidi giggled. "Not so tough now, 'eh? Yesterday you said it didn't hurt." She shifted and made a gagging face. "Ick. What's that smell?" She swallowed and pointed to the front dash. "That air freshener tastes like rotten fruit to me. Can you throw it out? Pretty, pretty please?"

I sat down, fastened my seatbelt and glanced at my two friends in the back seat. One teenie tiny fairy and the other a distant relative to the Hulk.

Seth plugged his nose. "Why'd you have to mention it?" It came out all-nasal. "Now the smell's overpowering me." His shoulders rose and he swallowed back a gag.

I laughed, reached down and pulled the pink and red strawberry scented little freshener off my fan vent and tossed it in the garbage can in front of my car. I started the engine. "I'd give anything to block out a sound – any sound."

Brent's eyebrows went up. "It's too much?"

Before I could answer, Seth leaned forward. "Last night's still lingering a bit. If I inhale deeply I can still smell the fire." He stuck his tongue out a few times as if his throat had been scorched.

Brent rolled his eyes. "Dude, I was asking Zoe."

Seth dropped back against the seat, making the whole car shake. "I sense that now." He chucked. "Get it? *Sense* that now? I totally didn't mean to say that."

"You're a funny man." Heidi voice came across, clear and sarcastic.

"Are you wishing it would go away?" Brent watched me intently and made a conscious effort to speak quietly.

"I don't hate it." I said to Brent as I tried to ignore the saccades loud buzzing from the tree's lining the street and focus on the road. "Look what we did last night." I winked at Brent. "Who'd have guessed we'd be water tower sliding like death-defying crazy tight rope walkers, and then stopping a fire!"

"It was pretty crazy." He grinned. "I'm not complaining about our new skills."

"I just wish they came with an on and off switch." I rubbed my left eye.

"That would be nice." Heidi giggled. "I'd even settle for a dimmer button."

We turned into Brent's driveway and headed around to the gym. Kieran's motorbike sat next to the entrance so I parked the Bug beside it. Everyone climbed out of the car and stretched. As we walked towards the doors I tried to stifle back a yawn.

Brent paused at the door, his hand resting on the handle. "You know what I just realized? Seth and Heidi have similar abilities. Kinda like Rylee and me." He shot me a sympathetic look. "I think it's different for Zoe...Like living with the volume on full blast with everything. You're sort of on your own."

Seth shrugged. "Guess so. Zoe's tough. She can handle it. Kieran should try and help you. Since he's got nothing, maybe he could take up some of the slack." He pointed at Brent. "What've you figured out with your ability? You're skills seem all jacked up?"

"Not reall. I think I've kinda figured them out. It's a weird sense of touch ability, but it's not like there's some manual to compare or refer too. My hands are like see through windows. I touch a wall and can see the other side. I play a guitar and it's like I own its strings."

"X-ray vision." Heidi tapped a finger against her chin. "Which is weird. It's like you've got sight inside your touch. Like two abilities in one."

Seth laughed. "At least if something happens to Rylee, we've still got all the senses covered."

Heidi punched in him the arm.

"Ow! What w—"

"Not funny." Heidi glared at him.

"At all," I added.

Brent tried unsuccessfully to hold back a grin. "Rylee's got super vision. I don't have that. I can just see through stuff with my hands...and my feet. They work too."

"Gross!" Heidi covered her mouth as if the mere thought might give her the taste of feet inside her mouth.

As if to remind me how little control I had, crickets increased their leg rubbing screech, electrical wires hovered like a swarm of bees and any other little distraction became something big.

Brent opened the door. "Let's go and see what Rylee and Kieran are up to."

The hallway inside appeared dimmed compared to the bright sunlight. Brent's dad had offices and other rooms adjacent to the gym so barely any sunlight filtered through the hallway. By the time we reached the short distance to the gymnasium doors my eyes had adjusted. Music blared out of the stereo making it feel like my eyelids were bouncing to the beat. Kieran and Rylee had been busy. They had rigged part of the equipment so it looked like an obstacle course. Rylee stood on the far side, setting gym mats on the floor so the Velcro lined up. Closer to us, and slightly hidden so I'd missed him on my first sweep of the gym, Kieran lay on his back tying something under an Olympic size trampoline. He crawled out when he saw us.

"Oiy! What do ya think? Still need to do that whole section but it's coming." He pointed to an area with just a ladder with things lying on each rung.

Seth walked over and slapped him on the back. "Great idea. What do you want me to do?"

Kieran pulled a sheet of paper out of his back pocket and showed the hand drawn diagram which amazingly resembled the gym. "What if we made a sparring area over on the mats Rylee's setting out? This way we've got a bunch of spots and don't need to change it up for a while. I was thinking of setting the ladder up and hanging stuff on it that would use as stuff to spar with."

"Time out. Time out." Heidi made a T with her hands. "I'm game for setting the gym up but I can't stay late and NO going outdoors. We need to lay low a night."

"I need to be home too. Loads of homework or my mom's gonna kill me." Seth held his hands out like he was holding a huge weight of books.

Heidi tsked. "Will your dad call our parents about last night?"

"He won't." Seth shook his head. "We talked this morning and he promised not to say anything. I told him you girls were shook up from being trapped in the mine and scared from that night at PHP. He agreed to keep it quiet." He chuckled. "Yeah, my dad's pretty cool."

"Thank goodness." Heidi smiled. She viewed the room and then snapped her fingers. "You know what? We should build some plyometric boxes over there." She pointed to a bare spot in the gym. "To do plyo training. My old gymnast coach was a huge fan of jumping up and over stuff."

"Great idea." Kieran nodded.

Something metal clattered together and fell by Rylee. "Sounds like someone needs some help." Seth winked and jogged away while I covered my ears with my hands.

"We've got wooden crates in storage we could use for the plyo's." Brent elbowed Heidi. "Come with me to grab a cart. You can show me how to set them up." They headed to the far end of the gym by the brightly painted orange door.

With my baby fingers I rubbed circles on the sides of my temples. My ears hurt from all the noise, especially the reverberating pounding of the base coming from the music.

Kieran's gaze travelled from me to the stereo. "Crap! I forgot. Sorry." He jumped up and shut the music off.

For a split second, there was peace and quiet. Then the rest of the world resumed its uproar in my ears.

Kieran shrugged. "I tried."

"Thanks, I appreciate it." I hated the mixed vibes my body kept sending me. One minute it seemed like I was on a one way street and the next Kieran seemed to be thinking the same thing. Shame I sucked at flirting. Needing a distraction from my thoughts and something to deafen the noise, I nodded to where Kieran had been working when we walked in. "Anything I can help you with?"

He held a screwdriver in his hand and tapped it against the open palm of his other. "I've been tryin' to think of ways ta help you train yer ears."

I nodded, loving the way his "r's" rolled when he spoke. *Focus, Zoe. Focus.*

"... an' I figured working with yer core balance would probably help everything. Seth made a good point yesterday 'bout that." He pointed to the place where he'd been under when we'd walked in. "I jimmied stuff around the trampoline kinda like a gladiator maze. Trap doors and everything." He scratched his hair near the nape of his neck. "Do ya wan' ta try it tomorrow?"

"Might have to wait a couple of days." I raised my arm and pointed at my elbow. "Don't want to rip this open."

"Oye!" Kieran gently brushed his fingers along the rim of the bruise. "That's gotta hurt." He leaned in closer. "It looks like the scabs starting to come off."

"I ripped it?" I twisted my arm, his fingers still grazing my bicep. It hadn't come loose, it actually had peeled away because it was heeling. Weird. The bruise still hurt but the surface was heeling incredibly fast. I wanted to see it closer on my own before I mentioned it to the others.

My face red, either from embarrassment or his touch, I glanced away from his piercing blue eyes. "It's fine. I should probably bandage it. Except my dad's always nagging about scabs needing air except it'll be gross if I ripped it off."

"Brent!" Kieran shouted, cupping his hands around his mouth to avoid shouting near my ears. "Do you have a first aid kit?"

"In the drawer below the stereo. Everything okay?" Brent called back.

"Yeah, we're good." Kieran winked at me. "Let me find something in the kit to protect that."

Shy but totally loving the attention, I let Kieran rub ointment and then bandage my elbow. I couldn't speak and thank goodness he didn't try to make conversation either. I didn't want to think except my brain wouldn't listen. It kept wondering if Rylee had talked him into asking her out or, if they'd already tried a thing or two under the bleachers. The thought made my face burn and I avoided looking at Kieran.

"Does it hurt?" Kieran's warm hand gently held my forearm. "Did I make the bandage too tight?"

Our eyes met and I couldn't look away. His brows pushed together with a small crease line forming between them. His handsome face with those piercing blue eyes sent butterflies into my stomach. If he liked Rylee I was heading into huge disappointment. I shifted my stare to the square patterns on the wood floor. "I'm f—fi—" I cleared my throat. "It's fine."

His grip tightened like a vice on my arm. "What's wrong?"

~ End of Excerpt ~

Radium Halos Part 2 Available February 28th, 2014

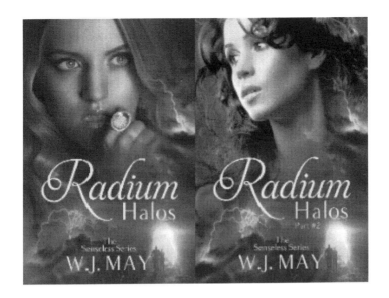

I hope you enjoyed Radium Halos. I love to hear from readers so please feel free to contact me or post a line or two review so others can find the series!

Looking forward to see you for part 2 !

W.J. May

MORE BOOKS BY W.J. MAY:

THE CHRONICLES OF KERRIGAN

Book Trailer:

http://www.youtube.com/watch?v=gILAwXxx8MU

BOOK BLURB:

How hard do you have to shake the family tree to find the truth about the past?

Fifteen year-old Rae Kerrigan never really knew her family's history. Her mother and father died when she was young and it is only when she accepts a scholarship to the prestigious Guilder Boarding School in England that a mysterious family secret is revealed.

Will the sins of the father be the sins of the daughter?

As Rae struggles with new friends, a new school and a star-struck forbidden love, she must also face the ultimate challenge: receive a tattoo on her sixteenth birthday with specific powers that may bind her to an unspeakable darkness. It's up to Rae to undo the dark evil in her family's past and have a ray of hope for her future.

** FREE CHAPTER EXCERPT **

The Chronicles of Kerrigan

Rae of Hope
by
W.J. May
Copyright 2012 by W.J. May

http://www.wanitamay.yolasite.com
Facebook Page:
https://www.facebook.com/pages/Author-WJ-May-FAN-PAGE
Cover design by: Patrick Griffith

The Chronicles of Kerrigan
Book I – Rae of Hope Book Trailer:
http://www.youtube.com/watch?v=gILAwXxx8MU
Book II – Dark Nebula Book Trailer:
http://www.youtube.com/watch?v=Ca24STi_bFM
Book III – House of Cards, coming March 2014
Book IV – Royal Tea, coming June 2014

RAE OF HOPE

Chapter 1

Guilder Boarding School

"You can't undo the past. The sins of the father are the sins of the son, or in this case, daughter."

Uncle Argyle's ominous words had echoed in Rae's head long after he dropped her off at the airport. "A proverb of truth" he had called it. Who spoke like that nowadays? *Some good-bye.* Tightening her ponytail and futilely trying to tuck her forever-escaping dark curls behind her ears, she looked at her watch, then out the bus window at the tree lined countryside. It seemed strange to see the sun. All she remembered was rain when she had lived in Britain nine years ago.

Trying to get comfortable, Rae tucked her foot up on the seat, and rested her head against her knee as she looked out at the scenery flashing by. A sign outside the window showed the miles before the bus reached Guilder. It'd be another twenty-five minutes. She popped her ear buds in, blew the bangs away from her forehead and stared out the window across the rolling farm fields, trying to let the music from her iPod distract her.

It didn't work. Just when she felt the tension begin to ease from her shoulders and she started to get into the song, something caught her eye. Black smoke billowed just near the top of a lush green hill. Rae stared, her heart fluttering as an old memory began to take hold. She knew what that smoke meant. She'd seen it before, long ago.

Someone's house was burning.

Crap, crap crap, no I don't want to go there. Her heart started racing and her stomach turned over, making her feel nauseous.

Dropping her knee, she gripped the seat in front of her, burying her face in her hands taking deep breathes, like the therapists taught her to do. She'd gone through years of therapy to treat what had been called "panic attacks". It didn't matter what other people called it. To her, it was simply hell; like being sucked back in time against her will, to a place she never wanted to revisit. So she breathed the way she'd been taught, slow breathe in, all the way, then slow breath out, all the time chanting *it's not real, it's not real* in her head.

It helped calm her racing heart and made her feel more in control, but it didn't erase the memory. Nothing on Earth could do that. Being back in England for the first time and seeing the strange smoke, Rae felt six years old all over again.

She'd been in the living room coloring with new markers before bed when her mother told her to take them to the tree house her dad had built for her and play there until she called her in. That call never came. The blaze bounced horrific shadows around the inside of the tree house. The stinky black smoke slithered in and scared her little six year old self in ways the monsters under her bed never had.

Rae shuddered and lurched upright, forcefully bringing herself back to the present. *Could this school be any further into the sticks?*

Glancing around the now vacant bus, she wondered if the driver had purposely left her until last. She'd watched the last few people get off at a school about fifteen minutes ago, Roe-something or other. They all looked the same, all pretty girls with blonde hair, not one of them thin, pale, and tall like her. They hadn't been friendly. *Big surprise there...* She was used to it. She tended to fly under the radar at best. So she handled them the way she always handled the ones who instantly didn't like her for no reason she could come up with. Rae avoided making eye contact and tried to appear immersed in the Guilder Boarding School brochure. It wasn't that she didn't want to make friends. She'd just never really had any. Most kids her age either didn't like her or didn't notice her.

It bugged her that Uncle Argyle had pushed so hard for her to go when Guilder sent the letter. He'd been the one to move them all from Scotland to New York when she'd come to live with them, taking her away from the horrible tragedy of her parents' death, and now, he suddenly leapt at the chance for her to go back? It didn't make any sense. It sort of sucked to leave her current high school. She lacked close friends, but she also lacked enemies, which was a plus in her book. The girls there seemed just as stuck up as the ones who'd gotten off the bus earlier, but they'd simply ignored her. Rae always told herself it didn't matter anyway. Cliques were *so passé* in her opinion.

Another weird thing that she couldn't seem to find an answer to was why Guilder would choose her? How did they even know she existed? Her uncle boasted how big a deal it was for her to be selected, but he'd never once explained how they'd even come to know about her in the first place. She had the grades, the brain part always came easy for her, but she didn't have any extra-curricular activities at all, nothing to make her stand out. So, how had this amazing school she'd never heard of before decide to take her on? It didn't make any sense. She tried a few times before she left to corner her uncle and get him to explain part or all of it, but he'd always seemed to be busy.

While this wasn't exactly abnormal behavior for him, it still left her with a sense of foreboding, something that had clung to her ever since she got the letter. She couldn't figure out why, but she had a strong sense that something big was coming. Whether it was good or bad, she didn't know.

A movement out of the corner of her eye caught her attention, pulling her mind out of the endless circle of questions in her head. She turned to look out the window, and was stunned to see the largest bird she'd ever seen in her life. *Maybe an eagle?* The thing flew parallel with the bus, right beside her. Pressing her face against the cool glass, her gaze focused intently on the curious sight. She jerked back when its large wings flapped, brushed the window, and then veered away. She watched its graceful flight as it soared and then swooped to settle onto the limb of a large tree just ahead. As the bus passed by, the bird seemed to lock eyes with Rae and she was mesmerized. Rae had always wondered what it would feel like to be a bird, to fly so free, go anywhere the wind took her. She continued to watch the bird until she couldn't see it anymore, then slumped back into her seat as the bus sped onward down the long road.

Guilder Boarding School. She gnawed at the cuticle on her thumbnail a little too hard and ripped the skin, drawing a wince from her. She couldn't help it, she always did this when she was nervous. She'd be the only American girl. *Well, not really American.* She held a British passport but had moved to New York after her parents died in the fire, leaving her orphaned. So...not really American, not really British; a little of both, but belonging to neither.

The bus cruised by an aged stone sign. *Guilder Boarding School, Founded 1520. One of Britain's Finest Educational Institutions.* Rae read the sign and wondered how a school could be that old and not be featured in stories or online. She found nothing when she tried researching it. They drove under an old, leaded window arch that connected two round, red-brick towers. The stream of people coming and going from the doors at the bottom made her think it must be some kind of office. She craned her neck to get a better view. The buildings were old but were well kept and held an almost magical aura of their original Tudor era. She half expected to see men in tights and codpieces strutting down the road, leading their horses, with corseted ladies perched delicately atop them. The mental picture amused her and she absent-mindedly smiled. Her eyes were drawn to the ornate, brick chimneys along the buildings' roofs. She glimpsed the other buildings beyond. *This place looks huge...hope I don't get lost.*

The driver pulled to a halt in front of a building with an embossed plaque that said "Aumbry House". The ancient building had ivy growing all over it. It looked like it was probably older than Henry VIII, leaving Rae with horrifying visions of chamber pots dancing in her head. *It better have indoor plumbing...*

The bus door slid open with a hiss. Rae gathered her two small suitcases and her book bag, clambered down the aisle and finally, blessedly, off the bus.

"Welcome to Guilder, Ms. Kerrigan." Rae awkwardly spun around to face the voice, finding that a tall, thin woman stood on the concrete steps of the building, her eyes darting left and right, pausing on Rae for barely more than a few seconds.

Rae stared, wondering where the lady had come from. *She wasn't there a moment ago.* Rae looked at the woman's long, wool skirt. *This might be England, but today is sweltering. How is she not melting in this heat?*

"I am Madame Elpis, your house mistress." The lady darted down the large concrete steps, pausing on the last step and, in one fluid motion, tucked her clip board under an armpit and extended her hand.

The woman's features reminded Rae of a bird – her jet-black hair, dark eyes, and especially the jutting nose. Rae nodded and dropped a suitcase so she could return the handshake, her fingers crushed by the woman's claw-like grip. *Ow, ow, ow! So you're freakishly strong, got it.*

"Come along. No time for dilly-dallying." She turned and marched up the steps, not checking to see if Rae followed or needed any help with her bags.

Huffing out a breath, Rae grabbed her things and clambered to follow, hearing the bus driver chuckle as he closed the door behind her. *I'm spending the next two years here? What joy; What freakin' bliss.*

Hammering and drilling noises from above greeted Rae as she came through the entrance. The clamor echoed throughout the building.

"Fifteen and sixteen-year-olds are on the second floor," Madame Elpis shouted above the noise. "Your room is the last door on the left." She checked the chart she'd been holding under her arm. "Molly Skye is your roommate. I assume you can find the way." The last part was more statement than question.

"Thank you," Rae replied uncertainly, not knowing what else to say.

Madame Elpis pointed to a door on her left. "The study hall's through there. The glass doors lead to the game room. The door to your right is to my living quarters. You are not permitted there." She led Rae to the winding staircase made of black and white marble. "Juniors are on the second floor, seniors on the third and fourth." She glanced at an old pocket watch hanging on a chain around her neck and, if possible, straightened even more. "Dinner is at five o'clock, sharp." She turned, her skirt swirling as she darted into her room, and with a kick of her boot, slammed the door.

Rae exhaled the breath she hadn't realize she'd been holding. The banging of hammers and screeching whine of electric saws reverberated through the hallway. She was so nervous, the hammering could have been coming from her heart and she wouldn't have been able to tell the difference.

Rae took her time up the marble stairs and, once on the landing, headed left to the end of the hall. Biting the inside of her cheek, she gave a light knock at the slightly open door and peered in. *Empty.* Rae cautiously pushed the door open and surveyed her new room.

Thick, lush brown carpet covered the floor. Two beds, with matching duvets and tan suede pillows, rested against the opposing walls. One of which already sat full of half-empty suitcases. Modern closets with ample space matched perfectly with the antique desks built into the wall by each oriel window. Rae inhaled deeply, taking in a mingled sense of fresh paint and the unique scent of antiques.

Finally! It'd been one helluva long day of traveling. Much of the tension ebbed from her shoulders and she cracked a smile for the first time in hours.

Rae dropped her suitcases on the uncluttered side of the room. Her roommate, Molly, must have stepped out halfway through unpacking. Her closet doors were spread open, with hangers already full of clothes and more shoes than Rae had owned in her entire life. She'd never been big on dressing up, but she still knew designer labels when she saw them and she saw an awful lot of them in that closet. Hopefully, her roommate didn't end up being superficial. Rae stood there wondering how she'd deal with it if she had to room with Guilder's Next Super Model. Visions of her roommate stomping up and down the room in heels practicing her "walk" distracted her. She didn't hear the footsteps walking down the hall to the door.

"What are you doing in me room?" Rae jumped and dropped her purse. A fashionably dressed girl stood in the doorway. She had dark, mahogany red hair, the kind women paid insane amounts of money to try to copy. *Oh great...well, here we go.*

"Molly?" Rae swallowed. "I'm your new roommate."

Molly stared Rae up and down. "You're Rae Kerrigan? I pictured someone totally different. You're not scary at all!" She laughed as if at some private joke. *Scary? Me? What is she talking about?*

"Name's Molly Skye. I'm from Cardiff, in Wales." She shoved one of her suitcases onto the floor and dropped into the small, open space on the bed.

Rae watched, confused. Why would anyone think of her as scary? Because she lived in New York? She had a terrible premonition of being the odd one out, and school hadn't even started yet.

"You're not sixteen, eh? No ta'too?" Molly pointedly dropped her gaze down to Rae's waist, as if she expected Rae to show her something.

Tattoo? Rae squinted, trying to listen closer to Molly's accent. The way she spoke, some of the words were hard to make out. *Why would she ask if I have a tattoo?*

"My birthday's in three days. It's going to be so awesome!" Molly leaned back on her elbows. "When's yers?"

"My birthday? Uh...not 'til November." *Straight into the personal info. Okay, I think I know what my roommate is going to be like.*

"November? You do have a long wait." Molly grimaced and shook her head. "Poor you. You'll be the last one inked for sure." She jumped off the bed. Rae noted the strange comment, but Molly's motor-mouth went speeding on, so she filed it away for examination at a later time.

"What'd you think of our room? Pretty cool, eh? Aside from the construction on the floors above us." She shot the ceiling an annoyed look. "I just talked to one of the workers. He said they finish at four. They start again at like eight in the morning! Can you believe that? Who gets up at that time, anyway?"

Wow. Molly can talk without pausing for breath. Rae nodded and tried to keep up. She watched Molly roll from the balls of her feet to her heels, back and forth continually. It was a typically nervous gesture that Rae attributed to meeting new people. *Everybody has their issues, but it's still surprising, considering how fast she's talking.*

"Can you believe we got invited to Guilder? We're two of sixteen females within a landmass of rich, supposedly unattainable, handsome boys." When Rae didn't respond, Molly squinted at her.

"You do know why you're here, right?"

Rae shrugged. Jet lag seemed to be eating her brain cells. "To be honest, I don't really know what you mean. I haven't been in England since I was six and I know nothing about Guilder." *Despite numerous Google searches at home and having my nose buried in the brochure for an hour on the ride here.*

"You're not slow or something, are you?" Rae shook her head slowly wondering if her talkative new roomie had just insulted her. Molly stared, scratching her head. "You really don't know, do you?" She looked up and to the left, obviously recalling something important. She straightened, as if quoting some bit of brochure from memory. "Guilder's a highly sought after educational institution, but it is primarily a school for the gifted. People who get to go to Guilder know why. The rest of the world has no idea!"

Rae curled her fingers tight, her nails digging into her palms. She felt stupid and also irritated at herself for feeling stupid. It wasn't something she wanted to deal with, especially after such a long day of travel. "What makes us...gifted?"

Molly's eyes grew huge. She paced the room. "Oh, my... Me da's never going to believe this. You seriously don't know ANYTHING?!"

Rae felt her blood pressure rising. She knew she was tired, confused, and nervous. None of that it was helping her temper, but she was determined not to lose it on what amounted to a total stranger. She pressed her lips tight to stop any snappish comment that might escape. *Can't the ditz just answer a simple question with a straight answer?*

Molly swung around in front of Rae, dramatically squared her shoulders, and put on a serious face. "When we turn sixteen, we receive our ink blot."

"What?"

"A ta'too." She leaned forward and whispered, "It gives us special powers."

Pause...say what? "P-Powers?" Rae tried not to laugh. Had her uncle sent her to an institution for the insane? "You're kidding, right?" Uncle Argyle had told her the experience would change her life, but hadn't said how. Rae figured he meant she'd do some growing up – like a maturity thing. And, of course, there was that silly proverb. But perhaps he'd mistakenly sent her off to a giant rubber room.

Molly waved a hand. "I'm serious. The gift is passed down from generation to generation." She blew out an exaggerated breath. "Any guy around here who's sixteen has a ta'too on the inside of his forearm." She dragged Rae toward the window and pointed to the building across from them. "That's the boys' dorm. Let's go outside and walk around. I'll get one of them to show you what I mean."

Her eyes dropped down to Rae's clothes, her lips pursed tight together. "Do you fancy a quick change before we go?"

Rae laughed, despite her roommate's serious expression. Molly definitely was crazy, but she had a point. She'd dressed comfortably for travel, and even though she wasn't big on fashion, even she drew the line at meeting her new classmates looking like a worked-over hag. She could use some freshening-up. "Yeah, give me a moment."

"I'm off downstairs to try and find some cute boys. Meet me outside when you're ready." Molly left, still chattering nonstop with no one in the hall to listen.

Rae opened the closest suitcase and grabbed the first pair of jeans and top within reach. She hesitated and dug a little deeper into her suitcase. The jeans were fine, they were new, but a white t-shirt seemed too plain. She found a pink Converse tank top with ONE STAR written in sparkles. She pulled out her hair tie, wishing her unruly black curls were straight like Molly's perfect hair. She never bothered with makeup because she had crazy-long eyelashes that mascara seemed to only want to clomp up against, and almost everything else just made her look kinda like a sloppy hooker. *Keep it simple*, that's what her aunt had always told her. She settled for lip gloss, and deodorant, and then grabbed a pair of sandals before tossing her purse under her pillow. *Now, time to find out what Molly's been babbling on about, or at least, maybe meet some cute guys.* She might be invisible most of the time, but eye candy was eye-candy, no matter which side of the Atlantic it was seen on.

Once outside, she shaded her eyes against the bright sunlight with her hand and searched for her new roommate.

Molly stood further down the sidewalk, talking to a very hot guy with chestnut brown hair, dark eyes and a dimple on his right cheek. It disappeared when he stopped smiling and began talking again, making Rae a little sad. She wanted to see that dimple again. Rae bounded down the steps, and then slowed down, trying not to appear too excited. She flinched and covered her head when a loud crashing noise sounded from above, and a large piece of debris flew down from the fourth floor and landed in the blue bin beside her. Face burning, she pretended it hadn't bothered her and continued walking. Molly and the boy turned to stare in her direction.

Rae heard someone holler from above, but couldn't make out what the guy said. Embarrassed by her reaction a moment before, she ignored the shout and kept walking. Molly's eyes grew big, her hands flew to her cheeks and her mouth dropped open. She screamed. Rae stared as Molly frantically pointed above her head. Rae tipped her head up. She froze in horror when she saw a huge, severed piece of wood paneling balanced like a seesaw on the window ledge several floors above.

The wood scraped against the windowsill, and teetered as if undecided which way it should fall. *Oh crap!* A gust of hot, dry wind blew by, knocking the severed beam into final decent. It spun as it fell and all sound was just gone.

Fight or flight. Rae dropped her gaze, her eyes darted about. The guy beside Molly moved toward her frozen frame. Everything moved in slow motion except for the guy running like a freight train. He was greased lightning, moving faster than anything Rae had ever seen. It didn't seem possible for a person to move so fast. *And why am I focused on him when I'm about to be squashed like a bug?*

Chapter 2

Proverb of Truth

Just as she was about to throw her hands over her head for what little protection she could offer herself, Rae's neck was jerked sideways, she went flying through the air and landed on dry dirt with a thump. Before she could react, warm arms wrapped around her body, forcing her head against a hard chest. They rolled together a bit and, and just as they stopped moving, Rae felt and heard the impact of the paneling hit the ground exactly where she'd been standing a moment before. Dropping her head back against the ground, trying to remember how to breathe after having the air squished out of her lungs, she opened her eyes and waited for them to focus. The cute guy lay on top of her, and the wooden beam had crashed down in the spot where she'd just been standing. The cute boy rolled off, but not before she got a thrill from the smell of his musky scent with a hint of delicious aftershave. *Wow...*

She stayed on the grass, unable to tell if being winded came from the fall or the boy. Rae spat some dirt out of her mouth and did a mental check. Nothing felt broken or even hurt too bad. Still dazed, she stared up at the building, trying to figure out if what had just happened was real. The shoulders and heads of two men in hard hats popped through the window.

"Everyone all right down there?" the one wearing a white hat shouted.

The boy glanced at Rae then called back up. "I think we're fine, but you guys are nuts!"

"Yeah, sorry about that. We're done for the day now, anyway." The men laughed and disappeared inside the window. Rae thought it seemed a bit rude of them, but had other more important things to focus on at the moment.

The boy dusted dirt and grass off his knees, then held his hands out to help her up. "I'm Devon Wardell."

Rae wiped her forehead, feeling dirt and grime mix into her skin. *Great first impression Rae.* She forced her attention back to the boy and nodded, her gaze drifting from his handsome face down his lean torso and along his bare arms. There, below the elbow of his right arm, lay a tattoo of a cute little fox with big ears. She blinked and sat straight up, silently pointing. Suddenly afraid all of Molly's crazy talk might be true, Rae didn't have the courage to ask.

"It's a Fennec fox. They're originally from the Sahara Desert." Devon's expression remained serious.

"You don't have long ears." Molly stated as she stepped over Rae to stand next to him. Rae could hardly believe the lack of concern for her well-being. *Gee, thanks roomie.*

Devon laughed. "No, I don't. Most of us don't actually take on the look of our ink." Shoving his hands in his pockets, he winked at Rae. He swallowed and then opened his mouth to speak, but Molly started before he had a chance.

"That's so cool! So, what's your gift? I mean, besides the speed thing we just saw. Did you figure it out right away?" She moved in front of Rae, blocking her view.

Devon sighed and sat down on the grass and Molly followed suit, settling next to Rae and actually leaning into her, making Rae wonder what she'd done to deserve having her personal boundaries invaded. However, it wasn't of the utmost importance at the moment, since Devon was again talking, flashing that dimple her way. "No, I didn't. The morning I turned sixteen, I had no idea of the tatù's power. My father's got almost the same one, but we never talked about it." He stared up at the sky and snorted, then he smiled at the girls.

"That night I figured it out quick." He gave a wry chuckle. "I got me some pretty cool nocturnal gifts."

"Awesome night vision?" Molly asked.

"Yeah, and incredible hearing. Plus, Fennec foxes can jump, and are super fast."

Understatement, Rae thought. *Speeding-bullet fast...*

"Fantastic!" Molly dropped to the ground and sat close to Devon. "I can't wait! Only three more days for me. My father's got some zigzag line, which he uses at his jewelry shop and a few other places he owns. It's like he's got a pair of jumper cables instead of hands! Hopefully, I'll have something more girly for my power."

Rae finally found her voice around the same time her brain caught up to the conversation. "Wait. Your dad's got a tattoo?"

Molly gave her a funny look. "Of course. Your parents bo–"

"Are you sure you're all right?" Devon cut Molly off.

Rae didn't miss the move, wondering what it was about, but was unwilling to re-direct his attention back to the conversion. "I'm fine, I think." She stretched her back. "Just shocked, that's all." Which was putting it mildly. *I just narrowly avoided death, and am now surrounded by people obsessed with tattoos who also have superpowers. Fantastic...Sure...I'm great...*

"Rae!" Molly turned, as if suddenly remembering the recent traumatic event. "Wow! You could've been killed! Glad Devon saved you, or I'd get stuck with some dolt of a roommate." She flipped her hair behind her shoulder. "What about you? Do you have any idea what yours is going to be? Any help from *your* dad? Or mom?"

Devon elbowed Molly in the ribs, but kept his concerned eyes on Rae.

"I...uh...my folks..." Rae didn't know what to say or think. Why would her parents have anything to do with this? Could what she was hearing even be remotely possible? Strange as it might seem, she knew it was true. It just seemed to make sense deep down inside, even though she couldn't pinpoint why. *Or...I could be going crazy...* Her stomach clenched and rolled. She suddenly felt woozy. "I...um...I think I need to walk around a bit and get some fresh air." She started to stand.

"Wait. I'll come with you. In case you pass out or something." Devon reached for her hand and helped her to her feet. Once she was up, he didn't let go, and Rae didn't want him to. "Molly, think you could grab Rae a bottle of water or something?" He smiled, and the cute dimple appeared again.

"Sure. I'll meet you guys on the front steps of Aumbry House."

Rae enjoyed the thrill from Devon's warm, strong hand in hers. She followed him down the sidewalk, concentrating on slowly breathing in and out. The dizziness began to disappear, but the dull pain of a headache beat at the back of her skull.

They passed a building marked Joist Hall. "I'm sorry Molly threw all of this on you. For the record, we aren't crazy. Headmaster Lanford told me you probably didn't know anything about our ink-art." He stared straight ahead. "The school isn't sure how much your uncle or father might've told you." He looked at her out of the corner of his eye. "Did you know they both attended Guilder?"

What? She planned to kill her uncle next time she saw him. She had obviously been owed a long conversation, stuffed with pertinent information, before he put her on the plane. *But all I got was a stupid proverb.* She shook her head. "Why do you know so much about me?"

Devon laughed and patted her shoulder. "You're quite the talk of Guilder at the moment—the English-American who convinced the headmaster, and dean, to open the college to girls." He coughed, as if trying to cover his words. "Or, uh...you know, open another college for females only...technically speaking that is...."

*Wait a sec...*Rae stopped in her tracks. "I didn't convince anyone! I haven't even spoken to the headmaster or the dean. One day I got a letter telling me I'd been accepted. I just assumed my uncle applied without asking me. He's originally from Scotland, so I thought maybe he knew about this place."

Devon waited a few paces ahead. "Weird." The puzzled look on his face turned to teasing. "Well, the faculty's pretty excited you came. You might not know them, but, trust me, they know all about you."

"What're you talking about?" She crossed her arms and felt the beginnings of annoyance emerge from her inner turmoil.

"You're special."

Rae's face burned. Giddy from his comment, she couldn't help but laugh. "No, I'm not. I'm just one of the average, quiet, sorta -smart girls. Though, at this moment, I feel pretty dumb." She tapped the toe of one sandal against the heel of the other. "Why in the world would the dean, headmaster, or anyone else think I'm special?"

"Because of *who* you are."

That didn't make sense. "'Cause I'm Rae Kerrigan?"

"Yes, silly, and because of your parents."

"What about my parents?" Rae could hardly remember anything about them. She'd been so little when they died in that terrible fire almost ten years before.

"I don't think it's my place to explain." Devon nervously shifted his weight from foot to foot. "Maybe you should talk to Headmaster Lanford."

"I plan to." She chewed on her nail, imagining some scary, crazy principal dressed in long, dirty robes who spoke in proverbs of truth like her uncle. "What's he...uh, like?"

"He's good. Big guy. Bad hair. You'll like him, and he'll answer all your questions." Devon absent-mindedly traced his tattoo with his fingers. "Don't pack your bags and jump on the first plane back to New York. Give Guilder a chance. It's even better than the brochures say." He grinned, showing his adorable dimple. "We'll grow on you. And trust me, when you get inked, you'll be glad you're here."

"On my sixteenth birthday, like Molly said? I'll get a tattoo on my arm?"

"Nah, yours is on your lower back." Devon's cheeks turned a light shade of pink. "It's way cooler on girls than guys."

Sexier was the word he didn't say, but Rae could read it on his face. She'd seen tattoos on girl's backs but never thought of them as anything more than ink. A tramp stamp. She needed to start taking notes if she planned to fit in at this school. "I guess I'll just have to wait three days and see Molly's." She had so many questions bubbling inside her. She wanted to ask if they got to choose their tattoo or if they were pre-selected for them. Maybe they had some kind of list. If there was, when did she get on it? She pressed her lips together, not wanting to appear denser than she was sure she already looked.

"Sure, or some of the older girls will show you." He pointed toward Aumbry House. "Molly's talking to Haley and Maria. They're both sixteen. Want to go meet them?"

Butterflies bashed around inside Rae's gut. What if everyone knew about her like Devon did? What did that mean anyway? She let out a slow breath. "Sure." No sense in being shy in front of the hot, and probably senior, boy. For some reason, she wanted to impress him and being a recluse wouldn't accomplish that.

As they walked back to Aumbry House, Molly ran over to greet them. The other two girls followed at a slower pace.

"Rae, meet Haley and Maria!" Molly gushed the introduction in what Rae was beginning to see was her typical fashion.

"Hi," said the blonde-haired, brown-eyed girl. "I'm Haley."

A tiny, dark-haired girl peeked around Haley's shoulder. "Hello."

Rae blinked. She could've sworn Maria had just said "hi" but she hadn't seen the girl's lips move. She glanced at the others to see if they'd heard it as well, but she couldn't quite tell. *Maybe it's the jetlag in my brain playing tricks on me.*

Devon checked his watch. "Ladies, I'd love to stay and chat, but I've a football match. My housemates will be ticked if I don't show. I'm already late." He patted Rae on her shoulder.

As he jogged away, Rae noticed the others staring at his retreating figure. *No surprise there. He's part superhero.*

"He's so hot," Molly murmured.

"And sexy. Definitely worth watching," Haley said. "And chasing."

"No dating, remember?" Molly half-heartedly chided.

"Guilder highly discourages that. It's taboo – not that I plan on paying attention to the that rule." Molly walked behind Haley and reached for the back of her shirt. Haley deftly stepped just out of reach.

Molly didn't even acknowledge the dodge. She just powered straight on into conversion. "Can we see your ink?"

"Have you figured out how to use it?" *Molly, definitely not the shy type.*

Haley laughed. "I, by no means, have mastered my gift. But I'm sure I've figured out what I can do. Coming here is only going to make me stronger and better." She pulled her shirt up and turned around to show her back to both of them. Above her jeans was a stunning tattoo of a whirlwind or tornado.

"So, what all can you do?" Molly asked as she impatiently tapped her foot.

"I can make wind."

Molly snorted.

Haley shot her an annoyed look. "No, silly, not *that* kind of wind. I create wind. Big wind, or even just little gusts." Haley twittered a high-pitched laugh which Rae found annoying. "At my old school, I used to send small gusts to mess up my teacher's piles of papers, other stuff like that. Right now, though, if I try anything stronger, I end up flying backward."

Molly skipped ahead to the next subject, seemingly unimpressed with Haley's power. "What about yours, Maria? What's your ink?"

Rae felt sorry for the tiny girl. She looked like she wanted to disappear. Rae decided to come to the rescue and end Molly's little impromptu inquisition. "Hey, why don't we head over to where Devon's playing?"

"And meet more cute boys?" Molly gave a little kid-like bounce. "Let's go."

The girls headed off to the sports fields.

Thanks. A soft voice spoke inside Rae's head, causing her to misstep, but she quickly caught herself. She glanced at Maria from the corner of her eye and nodded. When Maria smiled, Rae grinned. *Holy Cow! That really happened! She talked in my head! This school is going to be so amazing.*

Molly suggested they head to the middle of the sidelines, so they could see both teams. They sat down on the bleachers to watch. It didn't take long for Rae to figure out Devon was easily the quickest and most talented on his team. The boys seemed oblivious to the girls sitting in the bleachers, which Rae didn't mind. It gave her time to calm the butterflies in her stomach.

A boy on the opposite team dribbled the ball near his goalkeeper. In the blink of an eye, he'd passed midfield and streaked around a defense player. He took a shot on the net, scoring easily. Rae blinked and rubbed her eyes, wondering if she was seeing things.

"No goal! No goal!" Devon waved his arms in the air. "Riley, you know the rules. Only natural play—*no* gifts!"

"Give me a break! I can't help if my slow running is faster than everyone else's," Riley shouted. His teammates cheered and slapped him on the shoulder.

"You're not faster than the speed of light without your gift! No way can you argue with the laws of physics." Devon tapped his head and the other boys laughed. "Trying to impress the girls?" The guys started walking over to where the girls sat.

"Whatever." Riley scowled at him.

Devon bowed dramatically to the girls.

"Hey, I'm Riley." He stepped in front of Devon.

Rae noticed a tattoo of a cheetah on his wrist. That explained his speed.

"Gals, this is my team. Our keeper is Nicholas, our two defensemen are ..." Riley's eyes and mouth stopped moving when they came to Rae. He simply froze, staring at her like he couldn't believe what he was seeing. *Is it my hair? Is there something on my face?* She suddenly wished she could hide behind Haley. But no matter how hard she wished, she could see by the look on his face, the something which had stunned him to silence, was her. "You're Rae Kerrigan, aren't you?"

All laughter and jostling from the guys walking toward them stopped instantly. Rae swore all their jaws dropped open at the same time. Her temper flared from embarrassment and the stress of the day combined with the fact that she had no idea why everyone was acting so strange. Words rushed out of her mouth before she had a chance to think them through. "Yes, I'm Rae. I've no idea what you've been told about me, but let me assure you, I feel ten times more uncomfortable around you than you do around me." *You strange bunch of gifted people have no idea how terrifying you are.*

Devon came to her rescue. "Don't mind Riley. He may be fast as a cheetah, but he has the tact of a rat." Riley scowled at Devon's comment, but it broke the ice, and the boys laughed and relaxed. *They obviously trusted him. Hmm...cute, superhero, tactful and now, trustworthy...nice package.*

Molly piped up, "I'm not inked yet. My birthday's in three days. Rae doesn't turn until November fifteenth."

Rae stared at her roommate in shock. How did Molly know that? She hadn't told her. Molly had the date wrong. Due to a clerical error when she was born, her birth certificate showed the wrong date, but at this point Rae didn't really feel like correcting the mistake, since Molly shouldn't have known it in the first place. It suddenly seemed like a very good idea to make sure her true birth date remained a secret.

"So you're just normal 'til November?" one of the younger boys asked. "Poor you for the next few months."

Rae just stared mutely at him. *Poor me?*

"That's Brady. He turned sixteen four months ago, but he's been here since he was thirteen," Devon said.

"Didn't help him learn any skills on how to control his gift," a different boy teased. Brady just smiled and pushed his fingers at the commenter, who went sprawling backward.

"Brady can control wind, like Haley." Devon ruffled Brady's hair. A tall boy with his dark, almost black, hair tied in a ponytail, rested his arm on Devon's shoulder. Rae noted the confident, comfortable gesture. This was obviously one of Devon's friends and Rae decided she wanted to know all of his friends. She'd need to start gathering information since everyone seemed to have the details on her already.

"Hiya. I'm Julian. My talent is by far the most interesting. I can draw the future." He tapped his long, artistic fingers on his wrist. "I've just had a vision telling me it's half past four and Lanford's getting hungry. If we want to eat, we'd better start heading back."

The guys collected their belongings. Rae stayed close to the girls as they headed back to the school buildings. She felt uncomfortable about the impact her name caused but she didn't know what to do about it, or even the reason behind it. She was glad that Devon walked beside them, along with Julian, who seemed unfazed about her identity. Anyone behaving like a normal person ranked high on her good list at the moment.

About half-way back, Devon interrupted what had become a comfortable silence. "We'll see you shortly, at the table." He let his shoulder rub against Rae's. "We'll save you a seat." The guys headed into Joist Hall, and the girls continued to Aumbry House.

"Don't you think they're all super -hot?" Molly whispered as they headed up the steps.

"Dunno." She shrugged, caring more about information than boys at the moment. *The headmaster had better be at dinner tonight.* She wanted to get some answers to the millions of questions flying around in her head.

Chapter 3

Headmaster Lanford

Back in their room, Molly did a quick hair check and make up refresher. Quick wasn't quite the right word exactly. She needed half an hour to *fix* what, in Rae's opinion, already looked perfect. Then they headed back down the stairs to meet the other girls.

"If we're the only four here so far, why the heck does Madame Elpis wanna meet downstairs? She makes it sound so...mandatory," Molly whined as they waited at the main entrance.

Rae ignored the childish tone of Molly's complaint. "Do you know what her i-ink is?" It felt funny trying to talk as if she understood everything.

"Madame Claws?" Molly laughed. "Not a clue. Each professor, as well as the headmaster and dean, is inked. So we know she has one, we just don't know what it is."

Rae grinned. Molly could switch moods faster than a light switch.

Haley, followed by Maria, came down the black and white marble stairs. "I heard Guilder won't hire anyone who isn't inked," Haley said. "My father says the school may seem like any other prestigious college, but everyone who graduates from here does big things. They're all successful and make loads and loads of money." She paused to flash a haughty smile. "My father does very well and has big plans for me." Haley finished with a snobbish smirk.

"What're you gonna do with wind power?" Molly asked flatly, rolling her eyes.

"I'll find something, and I'll be rich," Haley's expression transformed from snobby to terrifying, making Rae nervous.

What's the deal there? Rae wondered if Haley was any relation to the Wicked Witch of the West. *All she needs now is the cackle.* Rae could just picture Haley all done up in the witch's black dress saying "I'll get you my pretty!" and had to turn away from everyone to compose herself so she didn't laugh out loud.

"Um, okay..." Molly held her hands up. "How? I don't get how everyone here makes big money, if we're supposed to keep these abilities hidden from the rest of the world."

Haley smiled, all BFF again and Rae made a mental note to stay out of her way. She might switch moods as fast as Molly, but for some reason, it was creepier with Haley.

Haley linked her arm through Molly's. "Wait 'til you get your ink. Then you an' I'll figure out what we can do. We'll be rich and nab us some even richer hubbies."

Rae wanted to gag. *Real Housewives of Guilder?* How lame could they be?

"Haley's not that bad. Her father was real disappointed when Haley inherited the gift instead of her younger brother. Seems the gift gene is usually passed to males, and there has only been a shift in the past, like, forty years. Some people still would prefer that boys get the gift rather than girls." Maria's quiet voice in Rae's head bore a hint of bitterness.

Rae shifted to dispel the shiver that crept down her spine. It felt incredibly strange to have someone else's voice inside her head. *Can she read my mind too?* She turned to Maria and half-smiled. The worried crease on Maria's face disappeared. *That's not a no...better find out the answer to that question.*

Before Rae figured out how to test the issue, Madame Elpis strode in from outside, her heels clicking on the marble tiles. "Ladies, one should not keep gentlemen waiting, especially at meal times." She turned and reached for a switch above the door. As she raised her arms, her blouse lifted revealing her ink. Rae strained to see over everyone's shoulders. It was a little bird, a magpie. Molly flapped her arms and made a sour face. The girls giggled, barely managing to suppress the laughter before Madame Elpis straightened and shot them a stern glance.

Molly straightened and whispered to Rae, "Madame Crow definitely has eyes in the back of her head." Rae thought to herself, *You ain't kiddin'.*

The girls followed Madame Elpis along the path, past Joist House to a smaller building set in the shadows. A plaque on the wall by the door proclaimed it Refectory Dining Hall. White with wooden beams throughout, topped with a thatched roof, it reminded Rae of a post card her aunt once got of a Cape Cod house.

The sound from inside the dining area was like a stadium full of screaming fans. But as they entered, all the noise and activity came to a standstill.

A very large man with an overgrown comb-over stood up from his seat at the front table. "Ladies, I'm Headmaster Lanford." He turned slightly and cleared his throat loudly. "Gentlemen, I'd like to introduce you to the new students at Guilder." He walked around the table and introduced the girls by name.

The boys clapped with each introduction, but hands froze midair at the mention of Rae's name. Boys leaned in toward each other; a murmur of whispers buzzed around the room.

Rae closed her eyes and wished the floor could swallow her up.

Headmaster Lanford seemed oblivious to the reaction. He simply told the girls to find empty seats. From the size of his belly, he seemed to be someone who didn't like to miss a meal and maybe had seconds and thirds to boot. *He probably pinches chips from other people's plates too.*

Devon's voice rang across the silent room. "We've got seats for all of you."

Rae was so relieved to see a familiar face, she nearly ran to him even with everyone staring. *Would hiding under the table be any less noticeable?* She settled beside Devon and stared at her empty plate.

"Hope you're hungry," the boy on her other side said. "I'm Andy." He reached for the water pitcher.

His sleeve slid up, showing Rae his ink. Dark ink detail in black, grays and browns displayed a wolf sitting on its haunches. Rae's natural curiosity over-ruled her discomfort with her surroundings. She couldn't stop herself from asking. "Do you have the characteristics of your tattoo? Like Devon does with his fox mark?" Rae dropped her gaze and scolded herself for sounding like Molly with the back-to-back questions. She worried she had probably just screwed up royally, and managed to make an already bad situation even worse. Surprised when Andy laughed, she looked up at him.

"No, I'm a shifter." He pulled his sleeve up all the way and traced the image with his fingertips, allowing Rae a better view. "Don't worry, I'm a good wolf. There's no need to be concerned for Little Red Riding Hood or the Three Little Pigs. They're all safe from me." He winked at her.

"Good to know." She laughed, liking his teasing banter. "Are there any other shapesters...I mean shiftsters...shape-shifters?" She cringed inwardly over her tongue-tied, stilted conversation. *Could I act any thicker?*

"One other." Andy pointed to a guy with a beak-like nose sitting further down at their table. "Rob. He shifts into an eagle. Lucky bugger gets to fly!"

"You're joking?" Rae glanced at Rob who sat across the table, disbelieving the long-armed boy could actually turn into an eagle. She thought back to the large bird on the bus ride and wondered if it could have been him.

"He's the only one at the school right now who can fly. It's pretty cool and unbelievable at the same time."

Rae smiled. "*Everything* seems pretty cool and unbelievable.

Trust me."

Devon leaned across Rae and grabbed the basket of buns. "Pretty much all of us here knew about gifting before we started, at the age of twelve. Plus our dads usually explained things prior to coming." He chuckled. "Kinda like Dad's '"facts of life"' lecture."

Not me, thought Rae. *No dad to do that for me. And Uncle Argyle was certainly no help either.* But she planned on getting answers as soon as she could. Now wasn't the time to feel sorry for herself so she pushed the emotion to the back of her mind.

Rae carefully schooled her expression to hide her feelings and focused on gathering information. "You've been here four years?"

Devon appeared happy to fill her in. "Yeah, the school's designed to give you three years to prepare for the gift and then another two to help educate you and train the gift. It helps you enter back into the 'real' world and do some good with what you've been given without revealing yourself."

"Quoting the school manual again, Dev?" Andy nudged Rae to show he was teasing.

Rae smiled and played along, but held her hand up, as if to try and stop her thoughts. "Wait a minute." she considered Devon's words. "So...you mean, you get this ability and the school helps you hone your talents," – she waited to see Andy and Devon nod their heads – "but then expects you to act like you're normal and hide it?" It didn't make sense.

Someone at their table coughed, and mumbled, "Like father, like daughter."

Rae gave a slight jerk to her head, trying to see who'd said it. She'd heard it loud and clear, even if they were trying to muffle the words. She glanced around, but no one seemed able to meet her gaze, all of them suddenly too interested in their plates to lift their heads. She didn't get the comparison, but knew it had to do with her. It sounded too similar to her uncle's last words.

"It's easier to hide it." Andy patted her forearm.

"Why? Wouldn't the government or the country want to know? They could stop bad guys, and surely, not everyone with this ink-stamp uses it for good."

A few more snickers erupted around the table. Rae glared.

It ticked her off that people would think her dumb for not knowing any of this. They'd all been raised in this world, and she had only just been shoved into it today. *They know so much about me, don't they know that too?* She turned to Devon, wondering why his face had turned beet red.

Andy cleared his throat. "What would you do if someone shape-shifted right in front of you? Or while you were on a plane, you saw the stewardess boil water with no kettle, just her hand?" He shook his head.

Devon piped in, "If we let our secrets out, could you imagine how scientists or military people would treat us?

Andy replied before Rae had a chance to open her mouth. "Crap. They'd hunt us down, shoot first and ask questions later. We'd all be a bunch of lab rats." He grinned. "Or lab foxes and lab wolves."

Devon tossed a bunch of pasta on his plate and elbowed Rae. "Don't stress about it. These are really cool abilities to have at sixteen, but as we get older, they get strong —"

"...And can become very scary," Andy added.

Rae shuddered. *Maybe that's the reason why Uncle Argyle didn't say a word about the real Guilder College. He didn't want to tell me that I'm a freak and I have to go to school with superkids.*

"Guilder just wants to teach you to appreciate the gift and use it to your own, and the world's, best advantage. Lots of famous people attended here. It's the reason King Henry VIII started this college in the first place," Andy said.

Rae sat back in surprise. *This goes THAT far back?* "He wasn't gifted, was he?" Nothing could shock her now.

Devon and Andy laughed before Devon replied, "No, he just wanted to find someone gifted to help get him a male heir."

Molly rolled her eyes from across the table. "He should've thought about not wearing those awful-looking tights, or maybe spoken to a doctor to learn it's the male who determines the sex of babies."

Rae glanced sideways at her, wondering if Molly realized yet that the science of genetics had not existed way back then. *If they had, good 'ol Henry wouldn't have needed a divorce, and England might still be part of the Roman Catholic Church.* She decided to ignore Molly's outburst. "I've got another question." "Hit me." Devon slowly pulled his eyes away from Molly. The corners of his lips were twitching.

Obviously, he's thinking it too, but won't point it out. Handsome and nice...great combo. He just keeps getting better and better! He was looking expectantly now and Rae's mind snapped back to her question. "You said your dad told you. What about your mom?"

"She doesn't know."

Rae had been about to hit him with her next question, but hadn't expected that answer and got sidetracked by it. "Huh?" "Dad's inked. He never told my mom. She just figures it's a tattoo from his teenage days. He told me the truth when I got the letter to come here."

Rae tried to absorb that, wondering which of her parents had a tattoo, or maybe if they hadn't died, if one of them would have told her about all this and sent her to Guilder three years earlier. The possibilities made her head spin, and it was only the continuation of the conversation that brought her back to the present.

Andy leaned forward, his voice slightly lower. "Only one parent's inked. Except in –"

"It's almost always the male." Devon shot Andy a look.

Rae didn't miss Devon's smooth attempt to cut Andy off and prevent him from saying something, and glanced back and forth at both of them. "What's the matter?" Her voice rose slightly and conversations around their table stopped. She turned her entire body to face Devon. "Why so secretive? Seriously, what could be weirder than what I've already found out today?"

He made no response. Everyone around them sat there with a wide-eyed deer-in-the-headlights look that people got when they were caught by surprise.

That's my look! I should be the one looking like that! Something doesn't add up. Something isn't being said and I have to know what it is. So she picked what she thought was a random response. "Does this have something to do with *my* dad?"

The entire hall became quiet. Everyone stopped eating. Rae felt hundreds of pairs of eyes focus on her. No one said a thing. Most expressions held dislike, others pity, which she couldn't stand. Devon's sympathetic face became too much to take. She stood, ready to go back to the dorm and pack her bags. *This is bullshit. All of it.*

"Getting a wee bit frustrated, Ms. Kerrigan?" Headmaster Lanford stood at the head of their table. He appeared calm, almost oblivious to the reaction of the other students. His eyes held understanding without pity. "Would you care to join me on a walkabout?"

Yeah, I have some questions for Mister Combover. "Fine, let's go," she snapped, and then hastily added, "Sir."

END OF EXCERPT

You can purchase Rae of Hope for FREE

Shadow of Doubt

Book Trailer: http://www.youtube.com/watch?v=LZK09Fe7kgA

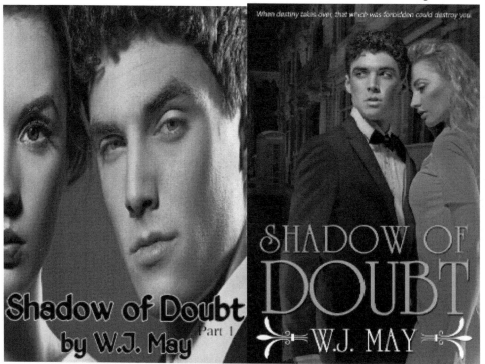

Book Blurb:

What happens when you fall for the one you are forbidden to love?

Erebus is a bit of a lost soul. He's a guy so he should be out to have fun but unlike the rest of his kind, he is solemn and withdrawn. That is, until he meets Aurora, a law student at Cornell University. His entire world is shaken. Feelings he's never had and urges he's never understood take over. These strange longings drive him to question everything about himself.

When a jealous ex stalks back into his life, he must decide if he is willing to risk everything to be with Aurora. His desire for her could destroy her, or worse, erase his own existence forever.

Free Books:

COMING SOON:

Book Blurb:

What if courage was your only option?

When Kallie lands a college interview with the city's new hot-shot police officer, she has no idea everything in her life is about to change. The detective is young, handsome and seems to have an unnatural ability to stop the increasing local crime rate. Detective Liam's particular interest in Kallie sends her heart and head stumbling over each other.

When a raging blood feud between vampires spills into her home, Kallie gets caught in the middle. Torn between love and family loyalty she must find the courage to fight what she fears the most and possibly risk everything, even if it means dying for those she loves.

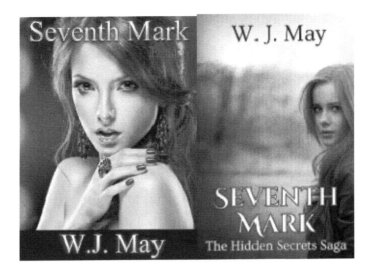

Hidden Secrets Saga:

Download Seventh Mark part 1 For FREE

Book Trailer:

http://www.youtube.com/watch?v=Y-_vVYC1gvo

Book Blurb:

Like most teenagers, Rouge is trying to figure out who she is and what she wants to be. With little knowledge about her past, she has questions but has never tried to find the answers. Everything changes when she befriends a strangely intoxicating family. Siblings Grace and Michael, appear to have secrets which seem connected to Rouge. Her hunch is confirmed when a horrible incident occurs at an outdoor party. Rouge may be the only one who can find the answer.

An ancient journal, a Sioghra necklace and a special mark force life-altering decisions for a girl who grew up unprepared to fight for her life or others.

All secrets have a cost and Rouge's determination to find the truth can only lead to trouble...or something even more sinister.

Did you love *Radium Halos*? Then you should read *Four and a Half Shades of Fantasy* by W.J. May!

Four (and a half) Fantasy/Romance first Books from five different series! From best-selling author, W.J. May comes an anthology of five great fantasy, paranormal and romance stories. Books included: Rae of Hope from The Chronicles of Kerrigan Seventh Mark - Part 1 from the Hidden Secrets Saga Shadow of Doubt - Part 1 Radium Halos from the Senseless Series and an excerpt from Courage Runs Red from the Red Blood Series

Also by W.J. May

Hidden Secrets Saga
Seventh Mark - Part 1
Seventh Mark - Part 2

The Chronicles of Kerrigan
Rae of Hope
Dark Nebula

The Senseless Series
Radium Halos

Standalone
Five Shades of Fantasy
Glow - A Young Adult Fantasy Sampler
Shadow of Doubt - Part 1
Shadow of Doubt - Part 2
Four and a Half Shades of Fantasy

Made in the USA
Middletown, DE
13 February 2016